SO SINGS
THE
BLUE DEER

CHARMAYNE MCGEE

A JEAN KARL BOOK

ATHENEUM 1994 NEW YORK
MAXWELL MACMILLAN CANADA
TORONTO
MAXWELL MACMILLAN INTERNATIONAL
NEW YORK OXFORD SINGAPORE SYDNEY

Atheneum
Macmillan Publishing Company
866 Third Avenue
New York, NY 10022

Maxwell Macmillan Canada, Inc.
1200 Eglinton Avenue East
Suite 200
Don Mills, Ontario M3C 3N1

Macmillan Publishing Company is part of the Maxwell Communication Group of Companies.

First edition
Printed in the United States of America
10 9 8 7 6 5 4 3 2 1

The text of this book is set in 11-point ITC Cheltenham Book.

Library of Congress Cataloging-in-Publication Data
McGee, Charmayne.
So sings the blue deer / Charmayne McGee. —1st ed.
p.   cm.
"A Jean Karl book."
Summary: Thirteen-year-old Moon Feather is chosen to join a dangerous pilgrimage to Mexico City to pick up live white-tailed deer, to be used to reestablish the natural population on Huichol land in the mountains.
ISBN 0–689–31888–X
1. Huichol Indians—Juvenile fiction. [1. Huichol Indians—Fiction. 2. Indians of Mexico—Fiction. 3. Mexico—Fiction. 4. White-tailed deer—Fiction. 5. Wildlife reintroduction—Fiction. 6. Wildlife conservation—Fiction.] I. Title.
PZ7.M4784625So   1994
[Fic]—dc20   93–26580

MAY YOU FOLLOW
THE DEER TO YOUR HEART

CONTENTS

CHAPTER ONE

FOOD OF THE GODS

Moon Feather bolted upright on his reed pallet. In the dark night, deer antlers loomed over him. Their needle-sharp points glinted in the moonlight.

He began to cry out, then realized he had been dreaming. The deer dream. It had come again. Always the same dream.

Wet with perspiration, Moon Feather sank back onto his bed and waited for his heart to stop pounding.

The deer antlers he had seen were real. They hung above him in the darkness, outlined in moonlight from the open doorway. They were suspended by leather thongs from the large wooden pole that supported the thatch roof of the house.

The antlers were real. But the stag in the forest had been a dream.

Moon Feather snuggled beneath the soft black bearskin covers. He peered about him at the familiar stone and adobe-mud walls of his family home. All his thirteen years he had awakened to the interior of this

Huichol Indian house, high in the remote Sierra Madre Occidental of northwestern Mexico.

He was safe, safe as his people had been since the Huicholes' ancestors had taken refuge in these isolated mountains centuries ago to escape their enemies—first other Indians, then Spanish soldiers who had come from across the sea.

Moon Feather could hear the sounds of the fading night in the black mountains outside. It must be early, he thought, for there were no portable radios blaring in the Huichol settlement. He lay listening for thunder— the voice of the god-spirits telling him that the blessed rains had come at last.

But what he heard was a mockingbird singing a rich, melodious song as she winged through the moonlight, "Whee see de tree tree." A coyote barked, "Yip yip yip," somewhere down the arroyo. He was headed home by way of the stony canyon after a long night's hunting.

It would be light soon, and with the light would come the most important day of Moon Feather's life. In a few hours, he would leave the mountains for the very first time. He threw off the covers, too excited to sleep any longer.

Today he, Moon Feather, must save the world.

He rose quietly from his pallet and slipped into the worn but freshly washed ceremonial clothes his mother had laid out for him.

His white cotton shirt and calf-length pants were embroidered from cuff to elbow and from hem to knee with red deer, orange flowers, green eagles, and purple jaguars. As the coarse cotton fabric slid over his skin, he felt the presence of the god-spirits wrap around him, warm and protective, for the embroidered symbols turned his clothes into walking prayers.

Each animal, plant, and bird, lovingly stitched by his mother, was a request to the god-spirits for a special favor.

The deer was a prayer for goodness; the flower, for rain; the eagle, for the protection of the gods. The jaguar . . .

Moon Feather bent to put on his leather sandals. He debated as he wound the long deerskin straps about his ankles. The jaguar meant either strength or cunning—he was not sure.

Guided by the moonlight leaking in between the walls and the thatch roof of the house, Moon Feather tiptoed across the neatly swept dirt floor.

He skirted the stone pit where his mother would soon build her cooking fire. Now it was filled with cold ashes. The smell of them hung on the damp, musty air and mingled with the spicy smell of dried *chile* peppers.

He was careful not to trip over her clay pots or the stone for grinding corn, which sat on the floor where she had left them.

His father, mother, and little sister were still sleeping. He could see the lumps of them as they lay under fur covers on the wooden bed platform in the corner. Their breathing was slow and rhythmic.

His baby brother slept in a cane cradle basket suspended from the roof beam, to protect him from crawling scorpions.

The thatch roof above his head bristled with ceremonial prayer arrows and bundles of eagle feathers. Their dark plumes stirred like bat wings on the shadowy ceiling. The feathers, fast and light, carried a person's most secret thoughts to the ears of the god-spirits. Moon Feather hurried his steps. He did not want the god-spirits to hear that his most secret thoughts were filled with fear.

Before leaving the house, Moon Feather stopped at the metal water pail by the doorway. He splashed the precious liquid from the bucket over his head and face as he asked the blessings of god-spirit Grandmother-Growth-Nakawé—she who makes the trees bud, who sends her gift of water to renew the earth. A little old woman with long gray hair, she paddles the seas and rivers of the world in a canoe. He prayed to her:

> *"Grandmother-Growth-Nakawé, Mother of*
> *Creation,*
> *You, who dwell in the waves of the ocean, falling*
> *rain, running rivers,*
> *Send us your tears of bounty.*
> *Make the earth green and renew our lives."*

He thought a moment, then added in a hushed voice: "And please, watch over us pilgrims on the journey we begin today."

As Moon Feather stepped from the warmth of the sleeping house, the chill morning air slapped him in the face. His wet skin tingled.

In the darkness, he left the cluster of stone and adobe-mud houses like his own and set off across the baked clay plateau. The landscape was bathed in the light of the full moon, and Moon Feather threaded his way easily among the nopal cacti and scrub oaks. Around him the night was alive.

Wind whooshed in the towering pine forests on the mountain peaks above the settlement, rattling green pinecones and whisking the fresh, crisp scent of pine to Moon Feather's nose. Those forests had once been home to Great-Grandfather-Deer-Tail, he had been told, in a time when the white-tailed deer were plentiful, and life had been good for the Huicholes.

But now the Huichol land was dying. Water was scarce; crops failed. The forests were disappearing, along with the game animals and birds that made their homes in them. The Huicholes were beset by illness, hunger, and poverty . . . and the rains did not come. Dead stubbly grass crackled beneath Moon Feather's sandals as he walked, a grim reminder.

The whole earth was dying. That was what his grandfather had said. For the Huicholes' pact with the god-spirits had been broken.

Beyond, in the dark night, the restless wind whistled down the stony canyons of the Sierra. The wind wailed on the craggy ridges above the black forests with a lost, lonely cry. Moon Feather shuddered.

The god-spirits rode the back of the wind on such nights, he had heard his grandfather say.

Moon Feather called aloud to them. "Do the people outside the Sierra understand? Do they know the world has continued to exist because for thousands of years we Huicholes have healed the earth and kept you happy with our songs and rituals?"

No one replied. His words were carried away by the wind.

Centuries before, Moon Feather's ancestors, the "healing people," had carved out tiny settlements on high plateaus in this land of bony mountain peaks nine thousand feet tall, rugged canyons a mile deep, and plunging waterfalls. The Sierra Madre—the "Mother Range."

Hidden from outsiders and protected by their isolation, they had risen each day seeking ways to maintain the balance of nature—to be kind to the earth, and make the earth well. They had worked with the creator god-spirits to assure that the sun rose and the rain fell. They had kept their family of god-spirits appeased by singing the ancestors' songs, performing the ancient ceremonies, and offering the sacrifice of the white-tailed deer that lived in the mountain forests.

But now there were no more deer.

The Huicholes could no longer perform the ceremonial rituals that perpetuated life and rejuvenated nature. The deer had been driven away. Great-Grandfather-Deer-Tail had abandoned them. And the end of the world threatened.

So Moon Feather and the other pilgrims were going to the city. They would walk for three days through the mountains, then go by bus to Mexico City, hundreds of miles to the south. They were going to bring white-tailed deer back to the Sierra.

"The deer is the food of the gods," his grandfather had said. "And with the deer's sacrifice, we sustain the world."

Now the god-spirits were hungry.

Moon Feather left the plateau and entered the dense woods. There the moon's bright light played among the fir and oak trees, casting eerie shapes that danced upon the earth.

"Shishiway, whooshiyi." The dark leaves murmured among themselves in the language they spoke before man formed words.

Moon Feather followed the path and soon he reached a moon-washed clearing. In the open space stood the *tuki,* the house-of-all-the-gods. The dark *tuki* sat silent, its shape outlined in a silver-thin edge of moonlight. Its peaked thatch roof perched like a ragged sombrero on the round stone and adobe-mud walls. Inside its windowless walls, it guarded the remnants of Grandfather-Fire that had survived the Great Flood.

Moon Feather could see a faint orange light glowing inside the god house. The open doorway beckoned him like a warm golden mouth.

He drew closer.

Above the door was mounted a round painted stone with a circular hole cut in the center. Ghostly light from the embers of Grandfather-Fire danced through the opening, the gateway between two worlds. There the god-spirits entered the *tuki* if they chose to confer with the Huichol elders.

"Shhhshshs, ssshshshseee."

Moon Feather froze. Was that swishing sound the god-spirits passing? Or had it only been the trees' pine-needled branches brushing together in the wind?

He stepped inside the doorway of the *tuki.* The god

house was cold and vacant now. The stone fire pit was filled with barely glowing coals. Grandfather-Fire was sleeping. But when Moon Feather had been summoned to the god-house the evening before, Grandfather-Fire had been an angry blaze.

CHAPTER TWO

GRANDFATHER-FIRE'S BLESSING

The night before, Moon Feather had entered the tuki and stood before the roaring bonfire of Grandfather-Fire-Tatewarí. Its great flames had snapped and crackled on a disk of volcanic rock, below which was buried a stone image of Grandfather-Fire. Smoke, the breath of the water gods, exhaled upward, escaping through a hole in the blackened thatch roof to return to the Sky Realm of the gods. Inside the god-house, the air was warm and stuffy with smells of wood ashes, burning pitch pine, close bodies.

The flames' dancing light had made phantoms of the Huichol Indian men who sat in a semicircle around the fire, their faces barely visible beneath their feathered sombrero hats. The colors of the embroidery on their clothing glowed in the firelight.

"Thum! Thum!"

Even now, standing in the empty *tuki*, Moon Feather imagined he could hear the deep, resonant voice of the *tepu* drum, which had spoken from the shadows as the *tepu* player struck the three-legged oak-and-deerskin drum with the palms of his hands.

Three shamans had been seated across the fire. The elderly Grand Shaman, the most revered Huichol shaman-healer and Moon Feather's grandfather, was sitting in the center, in his holy chair of bent cane and cactus fiber. He had been absorbed in discussion with the two assistant shamans who sat in low wooden stools to either side of him. Candles burned at their feet, which were clad in the palm-fiber sandals of the ancestors.

The Grand Shaman had appeared small and frail in the large holy chair. When he leaned toward the blaze, the firelight had etched deep wrinkles in his dark-skinned face. Below the wide brim of his palm-fiber hat, his iron gray hair swung in a loose mane as he gestured.

Occasionally, coughs racked his slight frame.

"Thum! Thum!" The *tepu* drum sounded.

"We must face reality!" The youngest of the three shamans had jumped to his feet with a shout, startling Moon Feather. He was Kükame, the "Silent One," but he had not been silent then. Moon Feather knew him because one of Kükame's five children was his own age—a skinny, unpleasant tattletale name Turtle Feet.

"Reality? The earth is dying before our eyes. That is the reality," said the Grand Shaman, his voice breaking with anger. "Man is destroying the earth. Does he not understand that when he destroys nature's creations, he destroys the finest part of his own being?

"Travelers bring word from distant places that the

oceans are being poisoned by man's inventions; the rivers are clogged with filth from man's cities. His factories sicken the air so that even breathing causes disease.

"Each day a nation of animals disappears forever from the earth. The forests are being destroyed and the land lies dead and infertile. Man, in his greed to conquer nature, pillages the natural world." The old man shook his head sadly.

"We Huicholes can no longer heal the injured earth. The balance of nature has been disrupted. Great-Grandfather-Deer-Tail-Marrakuarí has been driven from our mountain forests. The god-spirits refuse our pleas for help. They have turned their faces from us in anger, for we can no longer fulfill our pact with them.

"Father-Sun-Tau sears the corn in our fields; Grandfather-Fire-Tatewarí threatens to burn our forests. Grandmother-Growth-Nakawé refuses to send rain to bring new life from the soil."

Kükame paced before the fire. The firelight played upon the tall, thin man's cinnamon-colored skin and highlighted his beakish nose. It outlined his hair, which was short, for Kükame rejected the serpentine braids worn by Huichol men.

"Bringing a few deer back to the Sierra will do no good," he argued angrily.

The Grand Shaman sat tall. "With these first bucks and does, we will begin to repopulate the forests with Great-Grandfather-Deer-Tail's god-deer." He raised his eyes skyward.

"In my dreams, Kauyumari, the little blue deer who carries the words of the god-spirits to the shaman's ears, has told me that the god-deer must run again in the mountains."

Kükame had gone on to offer objections to Moon Feather's going on the pilgrimage, just as he had expressed misgivings about the pilgrimage taking place at all. Moon Feather could still see him, gesturing angrily. He could still hear Kükame's words.

"Moon Feather is just a child. There are others older and more deserving. No matter that he is the grandson of the Grand Shaman.

"There should be no pilgrimage," Kükame had beseeched the elders. "Turn your thoughts from these old ways. We must act now. The mestizo ranchers have petitioned the Mexican government to give them a large part of our land. Who knows what the government will say?"

The mestizos. Moon Feather was still puzzled as to why the mestizos would want Huichol land. Except for traders, squatters, and occasional farmers, few of those Mexicans of mixed European and Indian blood, whom the Huicholes called "the neighbors," ever ventured into Huichol territory. They lived many days' walk away in the lowlands.

Moon Feather had known a mestizo boy once. He was named Juan and he had come with his father to sell trinkets at a Huichol festival. Juan had given him a red plastic whistle on a silver chain. But Moon Feather's father had made him return the gift.

"The neighbors have always been our enemies," his father had said. "Nothing they offer is without cost. For the smallest things, we pay the highest price."

The Grand Shaman had had questions, too. "Why

would the Mexican government give the mestizos rights to our land?"

"We have no papers to prove it is our land," had been Kükame's reply. "If we agree to let the mestizos graze cattle on our grasslands and cut timber from our forests, they will pay us.

"Let them grow whatever they can sell in our valleys. They will pay us well. If we wait, we may get nothing. Our children are ill and dying. We need the money."

"Already mestizo ranchers overgraze our grasslands and draw off water from our rivers and lakes," the Grand Shaman had pointed out. "Mestizo squatters gnaw away at the edges of our territory and attack our outlying family ranches.

"With their powerful rifles, the mestizo hunters have slaughtered the deer and driven Great-Grandfather-Deer-Tail from our forests. Without the deer, the ceremonial rituals cannot be performed."

Kükame had whirled upon him. "We go without sandals trying to preserve our traditions, to perform the ancient ceremonies. And for what?"

The Grand Shaman had leaned forward in his holy chair and a feverish energy had shone from his black eyes.

"The sun was born into our world through the love the gods generated in the first ceremonies," he said. "The sun brought light and life. The gods created man to carry on that love.

"When the father-gods and the mother-gods left the earth, the gods created man to carry on that love, to ensure the continuance of that life by performing those same ceremonial rituals.

"When the father-gods and the mother-gods left the earth, they gave man the deer. The deer is life for everyone. The god-spirits asked only that we return their love by offering the deer's blood. That was our pact with the god-spirits, and now that pact has been broken."

The Grand Shaman pulled himself up from his holy chair and stood, holding the wooden rods of his authority.

"We have asked the Mexican government for twenty white-tailed deer. The request has been granted. My grandson and ten men have been nominated to go on the pilgrimage to Mexico City to bring back the deer.

"We must sing the songs Kauyumari teaches us, and conduct the ceremonies of our ancestors by sacrificing the white-tailed deer. Then the god-spirits will be pleased. They will help us heal the earth and renew their blessings upon our people.

"Moon Feather shall go on the pilgrimage in my place."

Kükame angrily looked each elder in the eyes. "And if I choose not to lead the pilgrimage?"

"That will be your decision." The Grand Shaman did not flinch. "You were designated to lead because you have made journeys along the same route many times. You know the city, and you are the most physically able of us three senior shamans. But if you choose not to fulfill your obligation . . ."

Kükame's tone turned cold. "Very well. I will honor the conclusion of the elders. I will lead the pilgrimage. But I will not be responsible for the boy's failure. Be forewarned!"

Moon Feather's spirits plummeted as he remembered. Why should he fail? To be chosen to go in his grandfather's place was the greatest honor of his life. He wished to be Huichol. Nothing could keep him from completing his sacred duty and justifying the faith his grandfather had shown in him. He would die first.

"*Eeee-a-ooooo!*"

Moon Feather jumped at the cry of a screech owl in the dark woods outside the *tuki*. Thoughts of the night before faded from his mind. He looked about him at the empty god house.

CHAPTER THREE

GREETING
FATHER-SUN

"Eee-a-ooooo!" *The owl hooted again as Moon Feather* left the *tuki* and set off toward the canyon where the Chapalagana River ran in the darkness.

Owls are omens of danger and disaster, he thought—birds of the night who lurk in the treetops while Father-Sun struggles for his life in the underworld, passing from east to west between the snapping jaws of the two-headed earth serpent.

I must be brave, Moon Feather told himself. He was a pilgrim now. He hurried along in the rocky terrain.

The wind whined in the lofty ponderosa pines, red spruces, and madrone trees on the mountain peaks. Moon Feather thought he saw a shadow stir among the rocks.

Perhaps it was a jaguar. But only the shamans could see jaguars now, for the cats had long ago disappeared from the high Sierra.

He was looking so hard at the shadow, he nearly tumbled headfirst over the lip of the canyon. He stood staring into its black gaping jaws. Like a green-feathered snake, the river, four thousand feet below, wound through the mountains—cutting Huichol territory in half and separating the five settlements.

Lush smells of wet and decaying plant life rose from the uninhabited river canyon. The valley was tropical and humid, far wetter than the plateau above it, for the hard clay plateau could not absorb rainwater. Most ran off into the canyon, which meant the Huicholes had to pray twice as hard for twice as much rain.

Moon Feather made his way to a ledge overlooking the blue-black mountain slopes above and the narrow river valley below. In the distance he heard the night voices of the Sierra animals. "Yip yipppeee-yip!" The coyote barked as he caught the fresh scent of rabbit in a moonlit arroyo. A wolf howled above his lair on a thicketed ledge.

For thousands of years, thought Moon Feather, the animals—like the Huicholes—had fought to draw life from the stingy, rugged mountains. Coyote, mountain lion, rabbit, black bear, blue wolf, and gray fox—and once, the white-tailed deer.

Moon Feather was weary of the daily struggle to survive. He was tired of being cold and hungry. This journey would begin a new life for him. The thought was thrilling, yet frightening.

Moon Feather looked up at the stars spread above him in a twinkling canopy. Were they the same stars that gazed down upon the lands beyond the Sierra? The lands to which he would be going for the first time in his life.

He thought of his uncle Wawameme, "Big Tree," who had lived in the city for twenty years. It was he who had first seen the god-deer in the Mexico City zoo.

In his letters Uncle made life in the largest city in the world sound exciting.

Moon Feather occasionally attended a nearby school run by nuns. He had seen photographs in the schoolbooks of tall buildings, and city streets filled with cars, trucks, and buses.

His uncle told him the city had more than fifteen million people, and more stores than a person could count, selling more goods than one could imagine. And there was something called "movies." His uncle had promised to show him everything.

Whisper, whisper—the rush of the dark river far below called to Moon Feather. The river, low now from the lack of rain, ran west to the Pacific Ocean. In a few hours, he and the other pilgrims would go with it.

In following the river, the Huicholes would have to cross the Line of Shadow. Moon Feather's heart pounded at the thought. The Line of Shadow was the boundary that separated the high Sierra where the Huicholes lived, called the Field of Light and Clarity, from the coastal region of the Pacific Ocean—the Kingdom of Shadows, home of the mestizos.

Once, when he was small, Moon Feather had asked his grandfather about the mestizo world outside.

"What lies across the Line of Shadow does not concern you," his grandfather had replied.

Moon Feather's father felt differently. He had seen some of the world.

"When the time comes, my son," he had said, "for better or worse, the gods will turn your sandals onto the path of your destiny."

The night sky was beginning to gray. Moon Feather could hear the songs of the day birds in the forest: the sweet warble of the mountain bluebird; the dreamy ghost songs of the russet-throated nightingale; the mournful *cuacoo-coo-coo* of the mourning dove. Somewhere a rooster crowed.

The cries of Father-Sun's day birds carried him up from the dark underworld and into the heavens to begin his daily trip. Father-Sun was coming now, rising in his shaman's chair into the rosy pink eastern sky.

Suddenly Moon Feather felt a hand on his shoulder. He jerked in surprise.

Moon Feather's grandfather, the Grand Shaman, was standing beside him. The old man's hand, brown and knotted with age like an ancient mesquite tree, rested on the boy's shoulder. It felt warm and strong as the brown earth on which they stood.

Moon Feather could almost imagine that his grandfather had gnarled roots for feet, roots that reached deep into Huichol soil.

"Today you leave," said his grandfather.

The two stood on the altar of Mother-Earth, watching the sun rise. Moon Feather smiled inside himself as the yellow globe of Father-Sun cut over the mountaintops. Its rays edged in golden light the thatch roofs of the distant houses. Mist like spun gold drifted up from the valley. Moon Feather had never seen such a beautiful morning.

"Look how alive Father-Sun is, how alive the whole earth is," said his grandfather. "The sky, the rocks, the streams—these are our great-grandparents, Moon Feather. They have so much to teach us, but they need our love in return." He paused, savoring the warmth of the sun's first rays on his weathered cheeks.

"Man must learn to trust nature again, my grandson. To recognize the healing power that lies in the forests and the mountains. The *kupuri* life force of Grandmother-Growth-Nakawé flows through all her creations, all souls are linked.

"Man must grow to feel in his own heart the pain of the wounded animal, the crushed blade of grass. He must learn to share the tears of every living thing."

"Grandfather," said Moon Feather. "Tell me about my name."

"Five days after you were born," began the Grand Shaman, "I dreamed your name, in the Huichol way.

"I saw a beautiful white bird soaring in the moon-light above the forests. A bird with feathers the color of the sacred rain clouds, the sacred deer tail. It was the white eagle-hawk, Young-Brother-Kuirro-Nuitse.

"The moon, Old-Grandmother-Metza, was shining in her third quarter, growing with the light of knowledge, but not yet knowing all. From that dream I chose your name—Moye' li Metzaya, Moon Feather."

Though he had heard the story often before, this time it seemed almost new to Moon Feather. Perhaps because so much was about to happen, perhaps because he was going away.

"For I believe, my grandson, that as the moon lights our mountain paths during the blackest part of the night and protects us from the God-of-Death-Tukakáme, so you will one day protect our people.

"With the mysterious wisdom of the feathers that rise on the wings of the birds—the feathers that see all and know all—so you will guide us Huicholes."

A deep cough, brittle as the sound of dry reeds

rustling, came from the Grand Shaman's chest. The cough worsened into a spasm, and the old man leaned on Moon Feather for support.

"Come, Grandfather," Moon Feather said, taking the old man's arm.

As they walked, Moon Feather vowed that on the journey to Mexico City he would leave offerings in the sacred cave of Grandmother-Nakawé as a prayer for his grandfather's recovery.

"Do you think the mestizos will seize our land, Grandfather?" Moon Feather asked.

The Grand Shaman looked toward the forested mountains. "The mestizos want our land, that is true. There is no escaping them.

"They fly over our mountains in their magic bird airplanes and helicopters. They send their words singing on the wind over great distances with their radios.

"They send men to teach us their ways by building schools that turn our children's minds against the ancestors' religion. They bring new beans to plant. We have beans. We do not need new beans."

The two Huicholes passed a grove of stunted avocado trees and paused at the corral in which the animals without souls were kept—cows, bulls, pigs, chickens, goats and sheep, mules and horses, brought to the Sierra by the Spaniards in the 1700s. The cows lowed softly, anxious to be milked.

Moon Feather was quiet for a moment.

"Is it true, what Kükame said? That the world does not care about the deer, about us and our traditions?" he asked.

"Ah, Moon Feather," sighed the Grand Shaman.

"There are people who mock us because they do not understand. They do not realize that we labor for the sake of the entire world. Man has fallen out of harmony with nature. There is illness everywhere. Cattle die, people die. There are doctors, and yet they die. Man has knowledge, but he lacks wisdom."

"But what can we Huicholes do?" asked Moon Feather. "We are so few."

The old man's eyes misted. "By restoring the god-deer to the mountain forests and performing the ancient ceremonies, we could restore the balance of nature, cure the illness, and rejuvenate the earth's powers to heal itself.

"The physical healing of our earth would be a spiritual healing for mankind as well."

Grandson and grandfather began to walk again. At last the Grand Shaman spoke.

"I have seen the vision of Kauyumari, the blue deer," he said. "The blue deer, messenger of the gods, who raised the newborn sun on his antlers to give life to the world. He who aids the shaman and teaches him songs.

"Older-Brother-Deer-Kauyumari told me in a dream that you are destined to become the Grand Shaman one day, Moon Feather.

"My bones are old now. Grandfather-Fire has lent me the strength to continue, but each season it becomes harder to stay awake all night and sing the songs of our ancestors until the throat aches, to dance until the sweat pours. I must leave youth in my place."

Moon Feather looked at the ground. He did not want to talk of his grandfather's passing. He did not want to become the Grand Shaman. He did not want to live a life of duty and denial. Was he not entitled to choose his own life? To see new places, experience new things?

"But I feel unworthy," he said.

"You will become worthy, Moon Feather. The gods do not care if our sombreros are tattered, or our clothes are worn. If our hearts are clean and good, they see us with kind eyes. We become their reflections, like a mirror."

The Grand Shaman continued. "This mission is your first test. Love requires a commitment of time and energy. We Huicholes must make this act of faith in going to the city to ask Great-Grandfather-Deer-Tail to return. We must show we are sincere in our determination to save the earth by restoring his god-deer to their homeland."

The steps of the Grand Shaman slowed. "Without the hope the deer bring, our people will lose faith. Our young men will continue to desert the traditions and leave to find new lives in the cities. Kükame will be right, the old ways will be gone."

"Yes, Grandfather."

The Grand Shaman patted his grandson's shoulder. Then the old man turned to walk back to his house.

"Come see me before you go," he called. "I must see you once more before you go."

CHAPTER FOUR

BUTTERFLY PRAYERS

The sun was up and it was getting late. Moon Feather was impatient to be on his way. As he ran toward home, he passed the small family ranches, which were bustling with morning activity. The women were already hauling water, grinding corn, and cooking breakfast. The smell of hot corn tortillas baking on the comal griddles made his stomach growl.

He ran panting up to his house to find his mother Pari Teami, "Beautiful Light," sitting in the yard, weaving a red-and-yellow sash. Her back strap loom was attached to a tree.

"Good morning, Mother," he greeted her.

"Good morning, Moon Feather." She smiled, but she did not lift her eyes. He knew this was the day she had dreaded for so long, for today her son passed from her world into the world of his father and she must step aside.

"I will bring your breakfast in a moment," she said.

Moon Feather stood watching her weave, memorizing her image to carry with him on the journey. She was so beautiful, he thought. Her thick black braids were wound around her head and tucked up beneath a red-flowered bandanna. She sat on the ground, her full print skirt folded around her. On her cheeks were painted red prayer circles.

Moon Feather watched her smooth, pale brown hands glide over the woolen threads of her weaving. She would spend hours like this, weaving quietly as time passed without beginning or end, a "bee without wings who stored the golden honey of silence," as his grandfather said.

She rose at last and went into the house for a bowl of hot boiled cornmeal atole. She returned with the cereal in one hand, a bundle wrapped in white cloth in the other.

"Open it," she said, handing him the package.

Inside was a beautiful new embroidered shirt. He examined it, gently touching the green, orange, and blue marching deer, the red eagles with outspread wings. Geometric designs and yellow *toto* flowers decorated the sleeves and yoke.

"It is beautiful, Mother," he said. "Great-Grandfather-Deer-Tail will be impressed when he sees what a fine shirt I wear to meet him."

"I am pleased you like it," she replied, her face flushing with pleasure. "The design came from the large rattlesnake your father brought me, the one he killed in the mountains."

"I think you are the best artist of all the Huichol women," Moon Feather bragged.

His mother gave him a stern look. "We must all—

women and men—work to complete ourselves, Moon Feather. Men and women must take pride in one another's accomplishments and help one another become the best that we can be.

"We must strive to create harmony and to be of one heart with all things. Once we set upon the path to do that, the god-spirits will guide us with divine inspiration. They will show us their designs."

She took his shoulder. "Now eat your breakfast. Hurry, or the men will leave without you."

Moon Feather ate quickly, then ran into the house and changed his old shirt for the new garment. Around his waist he wound the red-and-blue woven belt, symbolic of the serpent of Grandmother-Growth-Nakawé. Small woolen purses dangled from it. Then he put the triangular cape with its red flannel border over his shoulders. Quickly he tied his blue neck-scarf. He hurried outside.

"Good-bye, Mother." He threw his arms around her.

Then he was gone.

"Moon Feather!"

As he ran toward the settlement, he heard someone call his name. His grandmother was waving to him from the doorway of her house. Then he remembered—he had promised to see his grandfather before he left.

"Come here! Come here!"

His grandmother, in her long red skirt and pink-flowered cotton blouse, frantically flapped her arms like a tiny, bright-colored bird. Her gray braids bobbed up and down. In one hand she held an object.

Moon Feather sprinted up the path to her door. His grandparents' house was very near his own. But the houses were spaced far enough apart, as the gods had ordered, that the women would not argue.

"Good morning, Grandmother," he puffed, kissing her dark, wrinkled cheek.

She patted his arm. "Good morning, my grandson. I have something to give you." She took him by the elbow and pulled him aside from the doorway. "I do not want your grandfather to hear."

She held out a beautiful prayer bowl. It was made from a *tecomate* gourd, cut in half, dried, and covered inside with beeswax.

"I have spent many hours pressing these glass beads into the wax softened by the sun—to make an extra special design," his grandmother said proudly. "It is a prayer for your grandfather's health."

She turned the bowl gently in her hands. "See how beautiful the colors are? Color is like breath, for communicating with the god-spirits."

The bottom of the bowl was a glowing sun formed of concentric yellow and orange circles. Around the sun, in a pale blue beaded sky, danced five deer. Each one was a different sacred color—red, royal blue, green, white, and yellow.

Turquoise butterflies fluttered among the deer's antlers, and pink and purple flowers filled the sky.

Moon Feather studied it. "I hope that, as the god-spirits eat and drink from the bowl, they will consume your picture prayers, Grandmother."

The loose skin around his grandmother's eyes crinkled with concern. "Moon Feather, your grandfather is very ill. The Mexican doctor says it is his lungs. Your grandfather accepts that he has contracted a Spanish disease that our Huichol curing cannot heal." She shook her head.

"But I am a shaman-healer, too. I know he is ill because he has not performed all the proper rituals and made the necessary offerings to Great-Grandfather-Deer-Tail. Take this prayer bowl with you, my grandson, and leave it in the home of the Deer-God-Spirit when you find him in the city. Then," she added knowingly, "your grandfather will be well again."

She pressed the bowl into his hands.

"You will not forget?" she called out as he ran toward the door of the house.

"I will not forget."

Moon Feather burst through the doorway. His grandfather was lying on the bed. Even though the morning was already hot as noonday, the old man was covered with animal skins for warmth.

"We are leaving now, Grandfather," Moon Feather said.

The Grand Shaman stirred. "Come, sit a moment, Moon Feather."

The boy drew a stool up to the bedside.

"Where is my *takwatsi* basket?" the Grand Shaman asked.

Moon Feather found the rectangular basket of woven palm strips in which the shamans kept their most precious power objects.

The Grand Shaman opened it and removed the official letter with the eagle and snake seal of the Mexican government—the reply to the Huichol request for the white-tailed deer. Moon Feather had read it to him until it was dog-eared.

"Do you know of the Aztecs, Moon Feather?" he asked.

"The Aztecs were the Indians who ruled Mexico five hundred years ago," Moon Feather replied. "Mexico City was once Tenochtitlán, the capital of their empire."

He remembered seeing paintings in his history books of Aztec nobles dressed in white robes and golden sandals, wearing crowns of scarlet macaw feathers, and headdresses of rare blue-green quetzal feathers as long as a man's leg. Their golden jewelry was set with jade, emeralds, and rubies. On their shoulders hung mantles of green and yellow parrot feathers.

He remembered pictures of ferocious jaguar knights who wore uniforms made of jaguar skins and carried shields of stretched ocelot hide decorated with feathers. And eagle knights, wearing battle-dress costumes woven of bright-colored feathers, who carried wooden clubs set with shards of volcanic glass.

The Aztec women, their hair dyed purple, were shown being carried on litters by servants across the great white marble plaza, the Heart of the One World, beneath the towering Great Temple.

"Why do you think of Aztecs now, Grandfather? That was five hundred years ago."

"The Aztecs were very wise in the ways of nature, Moon Feather. Their early lives were hard and they were poor, but wherever they went, they used what nature provided them. They lived in harmony with the natural world.

"They will understand our problems here in the mountains. I want you to find the Aztec lords in the city and ask them to help us save our Sierra, help us restore the balance of nature and heal the earth."

"But the Aztecs were conquered by the armies of the Spaniard Cortés in 1521. If there are still Aztecs in Mexico City, why do you think they would have any influence?" asked Moon Feather.

His grandfather held up the government envelope.

"The Aztecs worshiped the sun and the rain—the eagle and the snake—as we worship Father-Sun and Grandmother-Growth-Nakawé, Moon Feather. Does not the national flag of Mexico display an eagle holding a snake in its talons? And see . . . official papers coming from the capital bear the same emblems—the eagle and the snake. The Aztecs were defeated, but they must maintain some share of power."

Moon Feather nodded. "Uncle did write in his letters that he and his family attend Indian dances held in the Aztec ceremonial center of the city. But what can Aztecs know about saving the Sierra?"

The Grand Shaman drew himself into a sitting position.

"Moon Feather, do you remember how the Aztecs searched for a new homeland for over a hundred years?"

"Yes," replied Moon Feather. "Their god told them to settle where they saw the divine sign—an eagle perched upon a cactus, holding a snake in its claws."

"At last the Aztecs entered the Valley of Mexico, which they named the 'Navel of the Moon,'" continued his grandfather. "The valley was filled by a great lake, called Lake Texcoco. On a small island in the center of the water, the Aztecs saw the divine eagle. On that island they built a paradise of colorful temples and beautiful gardens. Stories of its wonders came to us over the centuries, brought by traders and travelers.

"The Aztecs filled the city with exotic plants and birds, animals and flowers, from all parts of Mexico.

"Living in harmony with nature, they constructed a great dike and a system of canals upon which Indians in canoes carried their wares to the central marketplace. They cultivated the very surface of the lake itself by making floating rafts woven of reeds and tree branches. They covered them with mud dredged from the lake bottom, and planted them with flowers, squash, *chiles*, corn, and beans.

"The Aztecs created a vast empire. Tribute was delivered to the capital from subject peoples in the farthest regions—boulders of jade, vanilla beans, sacks of indigo dye, rare animals, seashells, and chests filled with gold, silver, and precious gems."

"And feathers," interrupted Moon Feather. "Our teachers said the Aztecs prized feathers. Their emperor Moctezuma collected the rarest animals and birds. His House of Birds was so big that three hundred people were needed to care for the birds and collect the feathers as the birds molted."

"Yes," said his grandfather, a faraway look in his eyes. "Travelers in the past told how Aztec nobles wore headdresses of rare blue-green quetzal feathers as long as a man's leg. Their artisans wove feathers into garments and fine tapestries.

"Feathers impart wisdom and bravery, Moon Feather.

So you see, the Aztecs must be a very wise people."

Moon Feather pondered a moment. "If there are Aztecs in Mexico City, Grandfather, I will find them."

The old man took Moon Feather's hand as the boy rose to go.

"You are a new pilgrim, Moon Feather. 'He who does not know, but is going to know.' I wish I could go with you to meet Great-Grandfather-Deer-Tail and to see the great city of the Aztecs. Remember everything, so you can tell me when you return." His voice fell. "My only dream is to live long enough to see the god-deer running once more in our mountain forests."

The Grand Shaman reached into his shaman's basket again. He handed Moon Feather a small glass prism.

"Keep this with you, my grandson. And when you are lonely for the mountains, raise it to the sky and Father-Sun will show you the Sierra."

Moon Feather held the prism up and looked through it. He saw not one, but five Grandfathers. He put the prism into his shoulder bag along with his grandmother's prayer bowl.

"Thank you, Grandfather," he said. "I go now."

CHAPTER FIVE

YOUNG-MOTHER-EAGLE SOARS

"Where have you been, Moon Feather?"

As he entered the central plaza, a group of boys ran to surround him. Stinging Scorpion, Reed Grass, Sound of Water, and Turtle Feet all talked at once.

"Tell us everything," said Sound of Water, leaping from foot to foot like a grasshopper on a hot comal griddle.

"I am going." Moon Feather tried to sound nonchalant.

"Are you excited? Are you as afraid as I would be?" asked Reed Grass.

"I will do my duty to bring the god-deer back to the Sierra," Moon Feather replied.

Turtle Feet planted his spindly legs in the path. "Well, I could have gone if I had wanted," he said indignantly. "But my father says the pilgrimage is no place for a boy. Man's work is to be done and a child would only get in the way." He pointed a bony finger at Moon Feather. "They will probably send you back the first day out of the settlement anyway."

Turtle Feet skulked off ahead of them, and Moon Feather noticed that the boy looked a great deal like his father, Kükame.

"Pay no attention to him, Moon Feather," said Stinging Scorpion. "We think you are brave to cross the Line of Shadow."

Everyone was up now. Radios blared from the houses, dogs barked. The pilgrims stood chatting among piles of supplies, water gourds, and bedrolls, while children chased one another shouting and screaming among the bundles.

The men were dressed in their best white cotton shirts and pants emblazoned with embroidery. The parrot, eagle, and turkey feathers on their hats danced in the morning breeze. Their sombreros were adorned with deer and squirrel tails, badges of honor indicating they had been on many previous pilgrimages. Moon Feather felt a sense of pride as he took his place among them.

He noticed the Huichol men were a mixture of shapes and sizes. Some were short and thick, with energetic round faces. Others were taller and thin, with high cheekbones and almond-shaped eyes.

Most were handsome men, like Moon Feather's father, Matzuga, "Beaded Wristband." Moon Feather spied him standing in the center of the group.

Moon Feather waved shyly to his father, and Matzuga nodded in recognition. He looked quite elegant in the clothing Moon Feather's mother had embroidered for him.

Moon Feather was happy, yet self-conscious, to have his father going on the pilgrimage.

Matzuga had been to the city many years before and he had not liked it. Moon Feather knew he did not want to return, but as the son-in-law of the Grand Shaman, he felt it was his duty. And his father was very strict about doing one's duty.

Moon Feather's heart was pounding. The men were ready to depart. Their wives, families, and friends were gathering to see them off.

"Moon Feather!"

The boy turned to see his friend Uzra Uri striding toward him. Uzra, "Wet Paint," was seventeen and the next-to-youngest member of the pilgrimage.

He smiled and waved as he made his way through the throng. Uzra, a head taller than Moon Feather, was broad chested and muscular, with a tapered waist and a thick mane of shoulder-length black hair. Uzra, Moon Feather thought, moved like a big cat, rhythmic and confident.

"Morning, Moon Feather," said Uzra, grinning widely. "Are you ready to go?"

"What are you doing with all those things?" Moon Feather asked him. "You look like a Mexican peddler."

Uzra was wearing five ceremonial palm-fiber sombreros, one stacked on top of the other. Each hat was elaborately adorned with squirrel tails, eagle and turkey feathers, and streaming colored ribbons. Little blue and red yarn tassels dangled from the hats' broad brims.

Uzra also had on three embroidered shirts, one over the other, and he wore several woven belts tied around his waist. Over his shoulder he carried a large pack filled with brightly colored Huichol art objects—yarn paintings, yarn and twig woven crosses, woven bags, beaded bracelets and purses, and miniature prayer bowls.

"I am going to sell these things in Mexico City," Uzra replied. "You know since my father died, my family needs the money. My mother and sisters and I have been working for days to make them.

"A friend told me that the Mexicans in the city will pay good prices for Huichol handicrafts. It is even better if you can find some foreigners. Tourists will buy anything and never argue about the price."

Moon Feather chuckled. "You are always looking for the short way, Uzra."

A sharp voice behind the boys cut Moon Feather's laughter short.

"You, carry this." Kükame, dressed in the finery of an assistant shaman, stood holding a heavy water gourd made from the hollow double fruit of the *tecomate* tree.

"It is full of holy water from Lake Chapala." His black eyes shot sparks. "Do not let anything happen to it, Moon Feather."

He shoved the twenty-pound gourd into the boy's arms and stalked off.

"I will take it," said Uzra, smiling. "There is always room for more." He tossed the heavy water gourd over his shoulder by its deerskin thongs as if it were empty.

"That is a nice shirt, Moon Feather," he said admiringly. "You should sell it in the city."

Moon Feather was horrified. "It was a gift. My mother made it for me. I cannot sell it without the permission of the woman who made it."

Uzra shrugged.

The middle-aged shaman had come in the Grand Shaman's place to bid the pilgrims farewell. He raised his hands for silence. He dipped the *muwieri* feathered wand to the four directions, then offered a prayer to the god-spirits for the pilgrims' safekeeping and the success of their journey:

"Fly, my prayers. Rise on the wings of the wind.
Fly, fly to the place of the rain message;
Soar through the blue space to your ears, o
spirits.
Guide the steps of our pilgrims, o gods, and
return them safely to this, their home,
This, the place of the rosy clouds."

Then he passed among the pilgrims, anointing them with branches of red orchids dipped in Lake Chapala holy water.

"Good luck." "Be careful." "Safe journey." "The ancestors and the god-spirits go with you," the people called as they waved good-bye.

"Now we go," said Uzra.

Moon Feather felt a strong tug at his heart. He looked for his mother's face in the crowd. She was there, smiling with pride.

His three-year-old sister, Tutú, clutched her mother's skirt. The little girl's big dark eyes watched Moon Feather from beneath straight black bangs. On her chubby cheeks were painted yellow suns, prayer signs to Grandfather-Fire for his safe return.

His mother held his baby brother in her arms. She waved the baby's fat little hand in farewell.

As the Huichol pilgrims set off across the dry, dusty

plateau, Moon Feather looked back. The small settlement stood behind him in the distance, surrounded by blue-green and violet mountain peaks studded with pine tress.

The tiny Indians were still waving.

Overhead an eagle flew. Werika Wimari—she who holds the earth in her talons and guards it, the center of heaven who bestows life. The protective spirit of Young-Mother-Eagle was with them.

A good omen.

CHAPTER SIX

CLOUD MOUTH PASS

The settlement disappeared quickly behind the pilgrims. Soon they reached the rocky crags at the edge of the plateau.

There the path climbed steeply upward amid jutting boulders, thorny cacti, and creosote bushes. The sure-footed Huicholes navigated the incline easily.

At the top, another parched grassland stretched before them. In single file, the Indians set off upon their mission to save the world.

Moon Feather became caught up in the promise of adventure as he strode along in the direction he had never been before. He tried to keep pace with the grown men.

The Master of the Arrows led the procession, carrying the shafts of knotty red brazilwood nailed with ribbons representing the colors of life.

Behind him came the Guardian of the Fire, bearing prayer arrows and gourds of sacred tobacco to clear the road of animals and devils. He also carried a stuffed deer's head, symbol of Great-Grandfather-Deer-Tail.

The pilgrims marched with great urgency, their heads inclined downward, arms swinging at their sides in rhythm. They looked like giant, winged dragonflies to Moon Feather.

The morning was already sultry, and the pilgrims' feet kicked up little dust clouds as they walked.

Moon Feather's spirits skipped with joy. They were on their way at last. Nothing could stop the pilgrims from fulfilling their objective.

But as the day wore on, and the sun blazed mercilessly down on them, Moon Feather began to tire. Powdery dust filled his nostrils and coated his tongue. He wanted to stop for just a moment, but the men kept up the frantic pace of the march.

Soon the absence of trees and the uniformity of the dry landscape began to bore him. Oh, to be a red-tailed hawk and soar over the mountain ranges, he thought.

But he had to struggle along in the way of man—one foot in front of the other.

The Huicholes, their faces obscured by the dark shadows of their sombreros, strode on, undaunted by the heat.

"I wish we could play a radio," said a voice behind Moon Feather. Uzra had slipped into step at his heels.

"You know Kükame has forbidden radios," said Moon Feather, turning to answer him.

"I know, but it is going to be a long trip."

Sweat had popped out on Moon Feather's forehead and was trickling into his eyes. He felt as if even his hair were perspiring. He wiped the salty streams away with the back of his hand.

"It is hot," he said.

"Sweating is good for you," replied Uzra cheerily. "It works the impurities out of your body. With your sweat, you pay tribute to Father-Sun." He grinned. "Grandfather-Fire says that you must work each day until the sweat pours, then you will live to a ripe old age."

Moon Feather noticed that the only sweat on Uzra was a few drops of perspiration on his upper lip.

Up and down the stony barrancas they went, through gorges that would be impassable torrents of raging, foaming water once Grandmother-Growth-Nakawé sent the rains.

The vegetation was as unfriendly as the terrain. Grizzled mesquite trees and prickly-thorned huizache bushes glowered at them. Cactus needles stabbed their sandaled feet, and scrub oaks barred the trail.

Moon Feather wiped the dust from his lips and took a drink of water from his water gourd.

"Save the water," called Uzra. "It will be afternoon before we reach the settlement of Santa Catarina."

Hours passed; finally the air became cooler and trees lined the path that ascended a mountainside. Above them, at the mountain's summit, a break in the rocks marked Cloud Mouth Pass, Jaikitenieh.

"There is no returning now," said Uzra. "Cloud Mouth Pass is the entrance from our homeland in the high Sierra into the Divine Realm, the Place of Our Temple.

"It is where the clouds of the east and west clash together. If the blue deer Kauyumari holds up the dangerous clouds with his antlers for us to pass, we shall be in a new land."

"A new land," whispered Moon Feather.

Higher and higher they climbed in silence. They left below them the leafy canopy of oak and cedar trees and entered tall ponderosa pine forests. Moon Feather had never seen such lushness. A green carpet of yew, wintergreen, and hemlock covered the forest floor. Yellow mushrooms, wild cherries, and cherimoyas offered a feast for deer—had there been deer.

The column penetrated the thick mist and the bracken ferns that obscured the path until they stood at the mountain's summit.

Kükame ordered them to stop.

The Master of the Arrows handed him two beaded prayer bowls filled with puffs of cotton that represented clouds. Kükame placed the bowls in a niche of rock, saying:

"Mother-Jaisinura, god-spirit of the white woolly
clouds that come from the east,
Jaiwiyema, god-spirit of the gray clouds that
weep from the west,
We salute you."

Going downhill was easier than climbing up. Soon the pilgrims were walking once more across a desert plateau where thorn-whipped branches of the ocotillo plant and spiny paddles of the nopal cactus stood sentinel. Moon Feather was getting hungry and tired.

In the distance he saw a cluster of tiny buildings. They sat on a grassy mesa nestled among deep canyons and red rock cliffs. It was late afternoon and smoke was already rising from the cooking fires.

"Is that Santa Catarina?" he asked Uzra.

"Yes."

"We will not stop, but will walk on until dark," shouted Kükame.

Moon Feather's face fell. "We are not stopping?" he moaned. His empty stomach rumbled against his ribs. His leg muscles ached from taking long strides to keep up with the men. But there was no arguing with Kükame.

The Huicholes knew that the shaman who led the pilgrimage guided their progress by trips of the soul. Each night, while he slept, his soul left his body in the form of a hummingbird. It would fly to where the pilgrims were to sleep the next night. In the morning, the shaman would remember the route and lead them to the appointed place.

"We will go west across the valley to the sacred caves, where we may ask the god-spirits' blessings on our quest," announced Kükame.

"Is he going to march all the way to the Pacific Ocean in one day?" Moon Feather muttered under his breath.

The Indians crossed the mesa of Santa Catarina and descended a trail that wound precariously down into a canyon. At the base ran a tributary of the Chapalagana River.

Moon Feather shivered, for the valley was filled with a damp chilliness. The high stone walls blocked the afternoon sunlight and flooded the gorge with purple shadows.

"I know these sacred caves," said Uzra. "They are places where the god-spirits transformed themselves into mountains and springs and caves. In these places they add their power to the earth, that man might learn from them. We go to trade our offerings for their power.

"One of the holiest places is the grotto of Grandmother-Nakawé. In it is a pool in which every Huichol is supposed to bathe once a year for good health and long life."

"My grandfather has spoken of it," replied Moon Feather, and suddenly he felt very far from home.

The pilgrims traced the stream westward, through a rocky passage dotted with waterfalls.

"Look ahead," cried Uzra. "That is the grotto of Grandmother-Growth." He pointed to the huge mouth of a cave visible in the cliff wall about two hundred feet above the riverbed.

The Huicholes climbed to the opening of the cave.

"Wait outside," Kükame told Moon Feather and Uzra. "The grotto is too small for all of us to enter."

The boys slipped inside anyway. In the dim light from the cave's entrance, Moon Feather saw a rivulet of water trickling toward the rear of the cave, where it formed a shallow deposit.

Around the edge of the pond, bamboo canes painted to look like snakes were stuck into the soft earth. Moon Feather knew they were symbols of Grandmother-Nakawé because bamboo was the oldest plant on earth, she the oldest woman.

As he watched Kükame place offerings before the carved wooden image of Nakawé with her white wool hair, he remembered.

"Oh, Uzra," he whispered, "I forgot to bring the offerings I wanted to leave for my grandfather's health."

"I am sure Grandmother-Nakawé will understand,"

replied Uzra. But Moon Feather was not listening. He was worrying about the forgotten prayer offerings.

Thank goodness I have my grandmother's prayer bowl, he thought as he felt for it inside his shoulder bag. I must see that it reaches the Deer-God when we get to the city.

Afternoon slipped into twilight as the pilgrims marched on. Dusk had settled when the weary Indians neared the place where they would camp for the night—Teacata, Oven of the Earth.

"See, there is the entrance," said Uzra, pointing to an ironwood tree at the opening of a honeycombed ravine. A stuffed deer's head hung on the tree's wrinkled black bark. It was surrounded by ceremonial arrows.

The pilgrims followed the arroyo to its end. On a flat space a hundred feet above a spring sat a miniature Huichol village. In the center was a child-sized *tuki* god house with a little thatch roof.

"Let's go inside it, Uzra," urged Moon Feather. "Kükame is too busy to notice."

Uzra had to stoop because the roof was so low. Among the dusty offerings inside stood a four-foot-tall stone image of Grandfather-Fire. It was smeared with blood and the ground around it was stacked with deer skulls.

"This is where the shamans come to pray for knowledge to cure," said Uzra.

"Moon Feather! Uzra!" Kükame called the boys. Moon Feather was glad to escape the statue's grimy gaze.

"We will spend the night here," Kükame ordered. "There is good shelter and water. Go cut wood for a fire."

Moon Feather and the other Huicholes dropped their bundles and fanned out into the desert canyon with their machetes. Night had fallen silently and swiftly by the time they returned with armloads of scrub oak, mesquite, and pine branches.

The Guardian of the Fire piled small pieces of damp kindling wood in the center of the cleared area below the *tuki*. He struck a spark from the flint he carried in his shoulder bag, and the sticks caught.

The men piled on the firewood they had gathered, making sure that each piece pointed north—north to their home beyond Cloud Mouth Pass, where the women of their settlement would be faithfully tending a huge bonfire in the village plaza. It was the beacon that would guide them home.

The women would continue to feed the fire until their men returned.

As the flames began to blaze, Kükame joined the pilgrims. He tossed a small piece of green wood into the fire.

"Rest your head upon this soft pillow, Grandfather-Fire-Tatewarí," he intoned. "You have eaten heartily of our offerings of freshly cut pine wood and oak. Now sleep, rest."

Uzra and Moon Feather sat watching the fire crackle.

"The yellow sparks are Grandfather-Fire's face paint," said Uzra.

"You, boy, bring more firewood. This will not last into the night." Kükame was standing over them. "Do not sit there dreaming, Moon Feather. Only a loafer gets more than he gives."

The young shaman stomped away. But Moon Feather made no move to rise.

"I do not think he likes you very much," Uzra said. "You had better be careful. He would be a bad enemy. They say a shaman can use his powers for good or evil. Perhaps he has already buried a black two-pointed arrow of sickness outside your house. Or one day, he might knock the *kupuri* life force right out of your head. Then you will be at the mercy of Tukakáme, the Vampire-God-of-Death."

Uzra spoke slowly and dramatically. "He is probably out there in the darkness now, just beyond the firelight. Waiting for a chance to devour you. Man is his only food, and he likes thirteen-year-olds best because they are still tender."

Moon Feather squinted into the eerie darkness. A shape hovered in the flickering shadows, but it was only Aikutsi, the barrel cactus from which rain clouds are born.

"Tukakáme is dirty and black because he never washes, and before he leaves for his nightly rounds, he anoints himself with the blood of his victims."

Leaning forward, Uzra whispered, "He wears the bones of his victims as a necklace. And when he walks, they rattle—like the sound of a rattlesnake's warning."

"Kukukua! Kukuka!"

Moon Feather turned in alarm as a shrill bird cry came from the dark canyon. It was only the cinnamon-colored squirrel cuckoo calling his mate.

Uzra stretched and yawned.

"Well, Moon Feather, you had better go gather the firewood now. You do not want to leave a 'not done that should be done.'"

Moon Feather measured the cold black night lying beyond the ring of glimmering firelight. He turned to Uzra with pleading eyes.

"Very well, I will go with you," said Uzra, laughing.

After a cold supper of tamales made without salt, so as to purify their bodies, the Huicholes settled in for the night.

One of the pilgrims brought out a violin crudely made of white cedar. Another tuned his guitar. Together they strummed a Huichol song written in the familiar five-note scale, the cry the god-spirits could not resist.

The melancholy music drifted up the desert canyon with the smoke from the fire as the round red moon, Aushiviriaka, rose over the distant mountains.

Moon Feather was very sleepy. He drew nearer to the campfire and cradled his head on his shoulder bag. The burning wood sizzled, releasing Grandfather-Fire's song in the flames. Grandfather-Fire-Tatewarí was the first singing shaman, guardian of the Huicholes, who protected them from the night chill.

Moon Feather lay listening to the lullaby of the desert. Crickets chirped; cicadas droned. "Poop, poop, poop," came the staccato whistle of the pygmy owl as he left his home in a saguaro cactus to hunt by the silvery moonlight.

The sweet desert perfume of early blooming yucca and Sierra night jasmine floated on the evening air like liquid honey.

The last thing Moon Feather saw before his heavy eyes closed was a falling star shooting through the jet black sky. The eagles of Father-Sun were attacking with arrows the snakes of Grandmother-Growth-Nakawé.

The constant and eternal combat: eagle and snake; dry and wet; death and life.

That was the way the Huichol world turned.

Moon Feather's sleep was troubled. The deer dream came once more:

> *A mountain forest of sunlit pines towered overhead. The forest was unnaturally silent. No birds sang; even the wind was stilled to a rustle.*
>
> *Suddenly a twig snapped, then another.*
>
> *A great golden brown male deer came crashing headlong through the tangled underbrush. His heart pounded in his chest; his nostrils flared at the scent of death snapping at his heels.*
>
> *As the buck ran, low-hanging vines snatched at his massive antlers and buckthorn bushes snagged his pelt, leaving little tufts of deer hair dancing in the forest breeze.*
>
> *The stag charged on, appearing and disappearing as a streak of gold in the shafts of sunlight filtering down through the tall trees.*
>
> *The sun gleamed on the deer's burnished pelt. Magically, the golden hair transformed into the coppery skin of a man, glistening with sweat.*
>
> *The runner's muscles strained as he ran. His palm-fiber sandals struck the earth with a dull, thudding sound. Deer, then man, then deer again. The enchanted buck raced on.*

His sides heaved from the effort of running, but he knew that to stop was to die. The wind carried the pursuer's scent to his nose, and the scent was getting stronger.

All at once the canyon ended. The stag stopped short, nearly slamming into a sheer rock wall ahead. The deer whirled to face his unseen enemy. The animal's eyes rolled in panic. Foam showed at the corners of his dark brown muzzle.

The deer's muscles tightened; he pawed the earth with sharp cloven hooves, then palm-fiber sandals, and once again hooves.

Bursting from the forest came a liquid black shadow. Driving, driving. It lunged toward the stag.

The deer lowered his antlers to charge. Their needle-sharp points glinted in the sunlight.

With a hideous cry, the shadow sprang.

CHAPTER SEVEN

THE LINE OF SHADOW

Before the sky reddened the next morning, the pilgrims had awakened and were ready to leave. As the orange-red ball of the sun emerged over the horizon, Kükame blew notes on a bull's horn, then raised the *muwieri* and sang a greeting to Father-Sun-Tau.

The young shaman's thin, treble voice lifted on the morning breeze and carried down the arroyo. The ancestors' songs Kükame sang seemed to spring from the very rocks, their bones; the red earth, their flesh; the coursing waters, the blood of their veins.

The ceremony was completed, and the pilgrims hurried to march before the sun climbed too high in the sky.

"Today we must make real progress," said Kükame. He glared in Moon Feather's direction. "Let no one hold us back."

The Huicholes retraced their steps down the ravine and joined the main streambed. As they walked, they passed a small cave along the river bank.

"Perhaps that is the magic grotto of Uteanaka, the

Goddess-of-Fish," said Uzra to Moon Feather. "She is a giant winged fish and she lives in a beautiful cave of colored crystal with her servants, the blue serpent Tatei Aik, and Shurakame, the fish who carries a light in his head.

"Shurakame leads the fish safely upstream, warning them not to nibble at our hooks, or play in our nets."

The Indians silently trekked on to the southwest—ascending mountains, descending into deep gullies, crossing dry mesas. First they followed the river, then they departed from it. At times the canyons of stone seemed to swallow them.

Kükame permitted them to rest little, for time was crucial. They must reach Mexico City at the appointed hour and return as soon as possible.

At last they descended a dangerous, twisting path to where the Chapalagana River ran five thousand feet below, widening on its way to the Pacific Ocean.

That day and into the next the Huicholes walked. As they moved south, the vegetation became more dense. The humidity from the river trapped the heat, making the valley muggy and uncomfortable.

Moon Feather had to stop to catch his breath, while constantly swatting giant mosquitoes that swarmed from the undergrowth.

"Oh, Uzra, can we stop just a moment?" asked Moon Feather.

The two boys paused to dip their hands and faces into the cool, clear water of the stream, drawing health and strength directly from the milk of Mother-Earth-Urianaka.

In still pools of water along the short, Moon Feather

noticed floating bouquets of fresh flowers, offerings left by passing Indians.

"We should be crossing the Line of Shadow before long," Uzra said.

Moon Feather had tried to forget. Soon they would be entering the Kingdom of Shadows, the mystical area of darkness ruled by the Sea-Goddess-Aramara—and home of the mestizos.

Aramara and her sea creatures lived in the Pacific Ocean near San Blas, beside the great rock Washiewe. The Huicholes made pilgrimages there to ask her to make the rain clouds.

Moon Feather began to watch the ground nervously. How far were they from the Line of Shadow? Was the daylight beginning to dim, or was it his imagination?

"Have we crossed it yet?" he asked Uzra.

"No," Uzra replied.

A short time later Moon Feather called out, "Have we crossed it now?"

"What?"

"The Line of Shadow."

"We crossed it back where that steep cliff stood," answered Uzra. "Why? Did you think it would be a black line painted on the ground?"

"Of course not," said Moon Feather sheepishly.

Knowing that he was safely across the dreaded boundary, Moon Feather relaxed. He felt no different. The land had not suddenly dropped off into blackness. He had not been eaten by large scaly creatures that breathed fire.

Actually, he decided, the world on the Dark Side was much the same as the world on the Light Side.

As the Huicholes neared the Pacific Ocean, they entered heavy jungle. The familiar oaks and pines of the Sierra were replaced by banana, mango, and papaya trees. The spicy perfume of jungle flowers, not pine, filled the air.

Moon Feather marveled at the wonderland of green palms and strangler figs.

Sometimes the vegetation was so thick, the Huicholes had to use machetes to chop a path. Kükame put Moon Feather at the front of the cutters, and it was not long before the machete raised blisters on his hands.

"You deserve a rest, young pilgrim."

Moon Feather looked up into the round face of his father's friend, Plant That Grows. The older man smiled and stepped in front of him. Soon jungle growth was flying in all directions from the chops of the experienced blade.

Moon Feather watched the movements of the man's broad back. Plant That Grows was agile for a man in his late fifties, a plump man at that. He wore his graying hair twisted back into an ancestor's knot, the style usually worn by the oldest Huicholes to honor tradition. The knot rose and fell in rhythm to the whacks of the machete.

"I have much experience at this work," Plant That Grows called over his shoulder. "Years spent harvesting tobacco and carrying heavy bags of coffee beans build muscle."

Moon Feather had heard his father say that Plant That Grows had left the mountains as a boy. He had traveled to many places and he knew much of the mestizo world. He had returned to the Huichol settlement only six months ago. No one had asked him why.

"Why did you come back to the Sierra?" asked Moon Feather, curiosity winning out over courtesy.

Plant That Grows did not miss a stroke. "Only the Huichol mountains can soothe my soul," he replied.

"Do you think the jungle is as beautiful as the Sierra?" asked Moon Feather. "I think there must be many places even more beautiful than the mountains."

Plant That Grows stopped chopping and stood up. His asthma, caused from breathing pesticides in the tobacco fields, forced him to rest.

"This jungle was once the most beautiful place I had ever seen," the man said, wiping his brow with the back of his hand. "When I passed this way forty years ago, it was a paradise filled with Grandmother-Growth-Nakawé's most marvelous creations. Like that *jamapala* tree." He pointed to a tree staggering under a weight of fragrant purple-pink tubed flowers. "There were *gambolino* and kapok trees," Plant That Grows went on. "Cypress trees hundreds of years old. And oil nut palms. There"—he gestured toward stumps overgrown with creeping vines—"grew ebony, rosewood, and mahogany trees."

"What happened to them?"

"Men cut them years ago for their fine wood. There were such flowers then also. Orange flame vines, and waterfalls of magenta bougainvillea. Orchids dripped from the tree branches in every color imaginable."

"Do you think the Aztec emperor Moctezuma had those same trees and flowers in his gardens in Tenochtitlán?" Moon Feather asked.

But Plant That Grows was thinking of other things.

"Ah, if you could have seen the many-colored birds, Moon Feather. Flocks of painted red, orange, yellow, blue, and green parrots filled the skies like rainbows with wings. Their chattering could be heard for miles."

"Moctezuma must have filled his House of Birds with those same birds," said Moon Feather. "Imagine having a cloak made of their beautiful feathers."

Plant That Grows smiled sadly. "Gone, the birds are all gone now. Killed—or sold by illegal traffickers. Especially the guacamayas, the red parrots, the yellow-headed parrots."

Plant That Grows's gray eyes teared. "And the animals—ocelot, jaguar, tapir . . . crocodile, manatee, sea turtle. Hunted by man for their skins, killed for sport, or sold to foreign zoos.

"Our Sierra may be the animals' last refuge, Moon Feather. Soon, it too may be gone."

Plant That Grows bent into his chopping again, leaving both Huicholes to their own thoughts.

"We will stop to rest for a few minutes," shouted Kükame.

The marching column halted. The men dropped to the ground and uncorked their water gourds. Uzra set down his heavy pack.

"Do you hear that noise, Moon Feather?" he whispered.

"What noise?" Moon Feather listened, then heard it—snorts coming from the jungle brush.

"Go see what it is," urged Uzra. "Up ahead, in that palm thicket, but watch out for snakes."

Moon Feather, tired as he was, forced himself to run

up the path because that morning he had missed seeing a jaguarundi. He had caught only a glimpse of the jungle cat's reddish brown tail as it disappeared into the foliage. He did not want to miss anything else.

Excitedly Moon Feather parted the palms.

"Eeee eeeeeeek!"

A terrible racket of squeals and snorts broke out as a herd of bristly gray backs charged at him. He had startled grazing wild pigs. They stampeded around him with angry grunts, then tore off into the jungle, leaving behind them a dank, musky odor in the air.

"You should have been faster. We would have had pork for dinner," said Uzra, laughing until tears rolled down his cheeks.

Moon Feather was not amused.

"Come on, let's catch a pig for supper!" Uzra, with the feathers on his five hats flying, loped up the hill and into the jungle. Moon Feather followed at his heels. "It will be easy to track them," he shouted, waving his machete in the air. "Follow the trampled brush!"

Near the top of the hill, Moon Feather lunged for a small piglet hidden among the ferns. The slick little swine slipped through his fingers, and Moon Feather fell laughing on the ground.

Suddenly a hand clamped over his mouth and Uzra whispered in his ear. "Be quiet and come with me."

The boys crawled to the rise of the hill.

"Look down there," said Uzra, pointing with the machete.

In the stony ravine below them, three-foot-tall plants with crimson flowers bloomed as far as they could see. The red blossoms bobbed above fuzzy gray-green leaves. Fat green seed capsules clung to the stems.

"What are those flowers?" asked Moon Feather.

"*Amapola*," whispered Uzra. "Opium poppies."

He shushed Moon Feather, gesturing below to where several mestizo men, wearing blue jeans and straw hats, were tying lumpy brown burlap bags onto waiting burros. Two men supervised the loading. Both held rifles, and one of them carried a pistol jammed into his belt.

A third man in a red shirt patrolled the perimeter of the ravine. He cradled a narrow-gauge shotgun in his arms. Occasionally he seemed to be looking skyward, toward the very ridge where Uzra and Moon Feather hid in the brush.

"What are those men doing?" asked Moon Feather.

"Collecting opium gum. See that man?" Uzra pointed toward a man stirring a large iron cauldron with a wooden paddle. "He's mixing the sap that oozes from the seed pods with water to make a pitch. The opium gum is easier to transport that way."

"How do you know that?"

"My uncles told me," replied Uzra. "They learned about these poppy plantations when they traveled the coastal states. Look there."

Uzra waved his machete toward a palm-frond shelter where a man stood at a table, patting out round balls of a soft brown substance. He weighed each one on a scale, then wrapped it in banana leaves. His assistant packed the lumps into burlap bags like those being loaded onto the burros.

Moon Feather leaned forward to get a better look. As he moved, a branch snapped beneath his elbow. At the sharp sound, the man with the shotgun jerked his head toward the rise and shaded his eyes with his hand.

"Uzra, your hats!" gasped Moon Feather.

Uzra snatched the tower of five sombreros from his head. Both boys ducked down and watched.

"Do you think he saw us?" whispered Moon Feather.

Uzra shushed him. But the man turned and walked out of sight beneath the palm shelter.

"Let's go!" said Uzra.

Moon Feather followed him away from the ridge and back down the hill. As soon as they were far enough away not to be seen, the boys stood up and ran.

"What do they want the poppy sap for?" asked Moon Feather.

"To make into narcotics," Uzra replied.

"Why are those men hidden in an arroyo on Indian land?"

"Because what they are doing is illegal. The federal narcotics police are searching for these poppy plantations to destroy them. That is why they have moved inland.

"Hidden valleys like these in our Sierra make good hiding places and the soil is fertile. Perfect for growing poppies.

"Did you see the metal cables stretched across the ravine through the treetops? Those are to snag and bring down the government helicopters when the agents fly in to spray the poppies with chemicals to kill the plants. They shoot any agents that survive the crashes."

"But why do they grow the poppies if it is illegal and so dangerous?" asked Moon Feather.

"Money," answered Uzra. "The heroin and morphine they make from the gum is worth a great deal of money."

The boys walked on.

"But yellow poppies grow wild near our settlement," said Moon Feather. "My grandfather calls them the prayer bowls of Grandfather-Fire. Sometimes he makes a syrup by cooking the poppy seeds and flowers with honey. He gives it to invalids who cannot sleep, or to people who have chest coughs."

"We Indians have always used poppies for medicine," agreed Uzra. "But my uncles say that overuse of the poppy causes people to act stupid. Sometimes they get dizzy and go into a deep sleep. They can even die."

"How can such a beautiful flower be so evil?" asked Moon Feather.

"The poppy, like the *hikuri* cactus that opens the shaman's ears to the voices of the god-spirits, are all nature's creations, Moon Feather. In themselves they are neither good or evil. It is how man uses them."

"Should we tell Kükame what we saw?"

Uzra shook his head. "No, not Kükame." He paused. "It is not our business."

The boys reached the other Huicholes just as they were getting up from their brief rest and preparing to move on.

"Where is the pig for our supper, Uzra?" teased the men.

Uzra smiled and shrugged as he replaced the machete in his belt.

"As I always say, I have never been a very good hunter."

CHAPTER EIGHT

GOLDEN SANDALS

One more day of marching would bring the Huicholes to the highway.

As the pilgrims neared civilization, Moon Feather noticed changes in the jungle. Fewer and fewer macaws, royal blue jays, or rose-breasted tanagers fluttered on colored wings among the treetops.

The animals became scarce as well. Moon Feather spied tracks occasionally, but now only unseen eyes watched the Indians from the deepest undergrowth.

The column followed the river once more, but its waters were muddy and sluggish. Plastic bags and aluminum beer cans floated by, and old glass bottles and garbage lodged in the shallow pools of water along the bank.

Great bare patches had been gouged in the jungle. Broken foliage lay brown and dying alongside freshly hewn tree stumps. Deep ruts remained where the trunks had been hauled across the soft earth.

"Forty years ago, the jungle stretched unbroken to

the sea," said Plant That Grows as the Huicholes picked their way along a path littered with smashed fruit and orange rinds, and sidestepped piles of burro dung left by burro trains from the nearby tobacco and banana plantations.

Eventually the pilgrims climbed a steep path from the tropical valley floor to the dry savanna plateau above.

"How desolate, how dead everything looks after the jungle," said Uzra as he surveyed the stubbly parched grass, the cacti, and the stunted scrub oaks.

Two hours later the Huichol pilgrims arrived at a mestizo village. It sat sweltering in the hot dust, just twelve miles from the highway. On that road they would flag down a bus to take them to Mexico City—and to Great-Grandfather-Deer-Tail.

The mestizo residents of the town did not seem surprised to see Huichol Indians come straggling down their dusty main street—even though one of them carried a stuffed deer head.

Moon Feather had never seen a mestizo village. He gawked at everything as the pilgrims walked along. The square, flat-roofed buildings were made of cinder blocks instead of stone and adobe. Moon Feather thought they looked like ugly, overturned boxes.

The men of the town, dressed in cotton shirts and blue jeans, lazed on concrete benches or sat on wooden crates in front of the stores, talking, laughing, and passing a bottle of tequila back and forth.

They watched the passing Huicholes silently, appraising them from below the shadowed brims of their straw hats. Here and there, Moon Feather detected the menacing bulge of a pistol under a denim jacket, the gleam of a pearl handle above a man's belt.

One man in particular seemed to watch Moon Feather and Uzra with curiosity. He was wearing a red shirt, and he seemed to be staring at Uzra's hats. A narrow-gauge shotgun rested on his knees. Moon Feather forced himself to keep his eyes straight ahead.

"Supplies? What supplies do you need? Candles, candy, batteries for your radios?" one of the mestizo shopkeepers shouted from the doorway of his store. "Your people know I have the best prices!"

A radio was playing inside the darkened shop. "Aye yee ayee." The ranchero music sounded good to Moon Feather's ears. He realized how much he had missed the familiar noise.

With dogs sniffing at their heels, the Huicholes continued down the street. They passed a butcher shop where flies droned in the noonday sun, buzzing about the bloody legs of beef that hung from the shop's rafters.

They passed a grocery store, which smelled of *chile* peppers, onions, and tobacco. Four mestizo men stood talking in front of the store as they watched white cotton bags of flour, beans, and rice being loaded onto their burros. They wore handmade clothes like the Huicholes' but without embroidery. One man had the largest black mustache Moon Feather had ever seen.

The men greeted the Huicholes with a silent nod.

Moon Feather recognized them as tenants of Huichol land. They often came to fiestas at the settlement. The Huichol allowed these "poor neighbors" to cultivate small farms on Indian land in exchange for half the crops they produced.

The tenant farmers were grateful, but found it no easier than the Huicholes to eke out a living on the stony land. The lucky ones had oxen, but most sowed their seeds in the Indian way—by digging a hole in the cleared soil with a pointed stick.

The Huicholes walked on. Next to the store was a faded yellow cantina. A line of gray burros stood tied to a wooden rail by the door. They nibbled stones in the dirt while waiting patiently for their owners to finish their tequila at the bar inside.

The burros were all loaded with lumpy, brown burlap bags.

Moon Feather nudged Uzra and pointed toward the burros. Uzra ignored him.

"Did you see the bags, Uzra?" Moon Feather asked as the Huicholes moved on.

"It is not our business," replied Uzra.

"No time to spend here," ordered Kükame. "We must reach the highway before dark."

"Oh, no," moaned Moon Feather. He could smell bread baking.

The Huicholes fell into formation and filed out of town. Behind them, a battered blue pickup truck rattled down the dirt road and pulled alongside the Indians. The burly tenant farmer with the big black mustache was driving.

"Want a ride to the highway?" he asked. He stuck his head out the window and Moon Feather saw that a fresh red knife scar ran from the man's left eye to his ear. The boy had not noticed it earlier.

"I'll take all of you for one price," the man added.

"We will walk. Thank you for the offer," said Kükame.

"Looks as though you've already walked," retorted the Mexican as he spit tobacco juice uncomfortably close to Moon Feather's sandaled toes.

Moon Feather looked down at his dusty, soiled ceremonial clothes with embarrassment. Wearing dirty clothes was against the orders of Father-Sun. There were scratches on his hands and feet, and he ached for a bath in a clear running stream.

"Don't know how you live out in those forsaken mountains, anyway." The man spit again. The red knife scar seemed to pulsate in the sun. "Accidents can happen to a man who doesn't watch where he wanders in that wilderness."

The pickup truck turned around to rattle back toward the village with the mustached man shaking his head and muttering, "No use trying to reason with Indians."

"Move on, move on," ordered Kükame. The pilgrims picked up the pace. By dusk they should reach the highway.

"There, there it is!" cried Uzra.

From the top of the hill, the Huicholes saw the mud-colored ribbon of road winding across the landscape. They reached it quickly and dropped their belongings.

"We did it," said Uzra, happily sliding the heavy pack of handicrafts from his shoulders. "We may have to wait hours for a bus, but at least we can wait sitting down."

Moon Feather's father came to join the boys. The

atmosphere became suddenly tense and formal. Moon Feather had had so little contact with Matzuga, he had almost forgotten his father had come along.

"Are you boys excited about seeing Mexico City?" Matzuga asked.

"Yes, Father." Moon Feather turned to Uzra. "What do you think the city will be like?"

"Big," replied Uzra. "Very, very big."

The sun began to sink low in the apricot sky. The men sat talking and eating the last of their cold rations of tamales and corn cakes.

A cool breeze wrapped like velvet around Moon Feather's tired body. In the waning sunlight, the hills took on hues of violet, green, gray, and turquoise. Blue rivulets of shadow ran down the sides of the distant Buzzard Mountains, where the Spaniards had once mined gold.

For over an hour Moon Feather anxiously scanned the horizon. Finally, a red-and-silver bus appeared on top of the hill.

Kükame stepped into the road and waved his arms to signal the driver that he had passengers waiting.

"I have never ridden in a bus before," said Moon Feather.

"Well, hurry along or that bus will leave you standing in the dust," warned Uzra.

The bus driver raced the huge motor of the bus impatiently as the Huicholes scrambled aboard with their bundles. They made their way to the rear.

Moon Feather slipped into the worn red plastic seat beside his father, taking this opportunity to be near him. Nothing had ever felt so good as the saggy, dilapidated springs beneath him. The other pilgrims sank wearily into their seats.

"I, for one, am grateful to cover the remaining distance on something other than my feet," said Uzra from the seat behind them.

The bus pulled away, swinging with a gentle rhythm. As twilight deepened, the bus groaned over the dirt road and finally joined the broad asphalt highway that followed the old Royal Spanish Road to Mexico City.

Outside the window, strange landmarks passed by. Moon Feather's eyes drank in everything.

"That tall mountain is the volcano Cerro de Sanganguey," explained his father. "It is extinct now. It has no fire left."

"Beyond the volcano is the deep blue crater lake of Santa María del Oro, where the Spaniards had gold mines. Your uncle and I went to see it many years ago on our way to Mexico City."

The highway descended sharply, past great dark rocks of hardened lava.

"Did you like Mexico City, Father?" Moon Feather asked timidly as the bus hurtled on through the gathering darkness.

"Your uncle Big Tree and I went there twenty years ago," his father replied. "I did not like the city then, and I know I shall not like it now."

"Why?"

His father looked out the window. "It was too big. There were too many people. I felt lost."

"What did you do there? Did you see any Aztecs?"

"Aztecs? I suppose so. We saw tall buildings and . . . I don't know." Father was becoming impatient.

"What did you like best?"

"Oh, Moon Feather, that was long ago. I think . . . I remember I liked the ice cream, and the girls. They were very beautiful in their short, gauzy skirts. But I was a young man then."

His father thought a moment. "I did like to watch the charros parade in Chapultepec Park on Sundays."

"Charros?" Moon Feather asked sleepily.

"Mexican cowboys. On Sundays they rode about the park on magnificent horses whose saddles were made of fine leather inlaid with silver. Their charro suits of soft brown suede were embroidered with threads of silk and silver, and trimmed with silver buttons and gold braid. Their sombreros had wide brims and were made of finest felt. They carried fancy pistols with handles of silver and mother-of-pearl."

His father began to relax as he recalled those days.

"The park in which they rode was really a forest—acres and acres of the most beautiful old trees, right in the center of the city. Tall cypresses as old as the Aztecs, magnolias, cedars—and jacarandas bursting with purple blossoms in the spring.

"Flowers grew everywhere—dahlias, red poinsettias as high as a man's head, orange Aztec tiger lilies.

"And deep in the forest was a beautiful blue lake with a small island in the center. Lovers rowed boats on the lake, and families ate their noonday meal on the grassy banks above it.

"I have never forgotten that park. There it was, a forest right in the center of Mexico City."

"How long did you stay in the city, Father?"

The bus was passing through the plaza of the village

of Magdalena. Glowing yellow streetlamps had come on in the tiny square. Young people strolled arm in arm around the wrought iron bandstand.

"How long did you stay?" Moon Feather repeated.

"Only two weeks. But your uncle decided to stay forever. He returned to the mountains only to marry. Then he took his bride back with him—your aunt Naurra, 'Certain Flower.'"

Moon Feather leaned his head against his father's shoulder.

"Your uncle made his life there, and I . . . ," continued his father. "I chose to return to the mountains." He paused. "Perhaps, perhaps I . . . "

But Moon Feather did not hear. The rocking motion of the bus had lulled him into a deep sleep. A dream sleep through which Aztec lords walked in golden sandals.

CHAPTER NINE

NAVEL OF THE MOON

Moon Feather opened his eyes. It was morning. Where was he? Had they reached Mexico City?

He pressed his nose against the window of the moving bus. Outside, dry stubbly fields zipped by. Gray-green patches of maguey and nopal cactus scattered over the stony landscape. Except for occasional buildings it looked much like the Sierra plateau on which the settlement stood.

"Good morning, Moon Feather," said his father.

"I do not see the city yet, Father. We have been traveling a long time. Are we nearly there?"

"We are still some distance away, but we will be there soon. I do not remember the city reaching this far into the countryside when your uncle and I came twenty years ago."

Before long, buses, cars, and trucks began to fill the highway. Many of the colorfully painted trucks were loaded with cargo—live chickens in little wire cages, cows, pigs, vegetables, sand, long rods of metal.

"Everyone seems to be racing to see who can get to the city first," Moon Feather told his father.

Then he realized.

"Of course," he cried. "Tribute."

"What?" Uzra, half-asleep, leaned forward from his seat and rested his elbows on the back of Moon Feather's.

"Uzra, these trucks are bringing tribute to the capital from the subject peoples, just as in Aztec times." His grandfather was right. The Aztecs must still be very powerful.

Moon Feather craned his neck to see if there were any jaguars or quetzal birds in the trucks, but they sped by too quickly for him to tell.

"Um," mumbled Uzra.

As time passed and the bus neared the outskirts of the city, the landscape was not what Moon Feather expected.

Everything was drained of color, bleak, and crowded. He saw no rich green mountains or broad blue lakes like Lake Texcoco, no fine palaces of polished white marble or gaily stuccoed pyramids.

Instead, the bus passed thousands of tiny gray rabbit-hutch houses that clawed their way up one rocky hillside after another. Dry brown grasses and dusty weeds lined the road. Only hardy survivors like the peppertree remained green.

"The city of the Aztecs must still be far away," Moon Feather decided.

The bus careened past factories whose tall smokestacks belched billowing clouds of gray-white smoke.

"Do you think Grandmother-Growth-Nakawé will be

jealous when she learns the mestizo city people have factories to make their own rain clouds?" Moon Feather asked.

The bus windows were closed, but he became aware of a strange, metallic odor that seeped in through the cracks and stung his eyes.

"Phew, what is that smell?" asked Uzra.

"The perfume of the city," answered Plant That Grows. He was sitting across the aisle.

"I am sure I would have remembered such a smell from twenty years ago," said Moon Feather's father, wrinkling his nose.

The sickly sunlight outside the bus became even dimmer, and some cars turned on their headlights as if it were dusk. Moon Feather's nose began to run. His lungs hurt with every breath he took. Something was very strange.

"Where is the sun?" he asked as he looked at the gray-brown sky above the traffic. "Where is Father-Sun? He was with us when we left the Sierra. Does he rise at a different time in Mexico City?"

"No," answered his father. "It has been morning for several hours."

"The skies above the city are always like this," explained Plant That Grows. "I have been to Mexico City many times, and I have yet to see the sun shine here. The air is so filthy with dust, factory smoke, and exhaust from the cars, the sunlight can barely penetrate it."

Just then the bus passed a school where children played outside in a concrete yard. "The children of the city paint only gray and black skies in their pictures," said Plant That Grows. "Many do not even know that the sky is meant to be blue."

"The sky is never blue here? The gray air never goes away?" Moon Feather asked in disbelief.

"Almost never—day or night. Only if there comes a heavy rain or a strong wind. A whole generation of children your age, Moon Feather, have never seen stars in the sky at night."

Moon Feather tried to picture a black night sky without stars. The only time the Huichol went to sleep without a blanket of stars covering them was in the rainy season.

"Then there is no moon either?" he asked.

"No, no moon."

As they entered deeper into the city, the bus passed great tall buildings, glass-eyed towers of concrete and steel. The hard, cold spires thrust defiantly upward, as if the men who built them were trying to pierce the sky and elevate themselves to the realm of the god-spirits.

Moon Feather had never seen tall buildings. The Huichol structures he knew were made of natural materials, like mud and stone. They hugged the earth, and were warm and protecting.

The city began to press in upon him. Trucks and automobiles choked the highway. He couldn't breathe for the horrible odor. The racket of honking horns, screaming sirens, and screeching radios assaulted his ears.

Still Moon Feather held out hope. He strained to catch a sight of the Aztec ceremonial center, and wide canals where flower-covered canoes carried tribute toward the marketplace. But he saw no trace of them.

Swish, swrush. Hurry, hurry. Cars raced by. Hhhmmmup, hhhmmmup—the bus tires hummed on the pavement, faster and faster.

Moon Feather felt as if he were a leaf fallen into a rushing brook of wet-season rains. Helpless, he was being swept along in the current of traffic. It was as if people, buses, cars, trucks, and their cargoes were being sucked into the center of a great whirlpool.

Where was Great-Grandfather-Deer-Tail?

At last the pace of the bus slowed, and Moon Feather calmed down. He began to notice the city people walking alongside the road. They were dressed in the same machine-made clothing the mestizos wore when they came to the mountains.

Moon Feather looked down at his own new shirt, so lovingly embroidered by his mother's hands. He ran his fingers over the prancing blue and green deer.

How would the Huicholes ever find Great-Grandfather-Deer-Tail in this maze of city stone?

"Look at the people," said Uzra.

If these city people were Aztecs, they certainly looked nothing like the Aztecs Moon Feather had expected. Some of them had very pale faces; others were very dark. Their hair was of different colors— black, brown, red, yellow.

"I do not see one lordly-looking man with a fine headdress of quetzal feathers among them," Moon Feather told Uzra.

"There is the station!" said Plant That Grows.

Over the tops of the crowded buildings, Moon Feather saw what looked like a gleaming white pyramid. Tenochtitlán at last. In the sunlight, the sloping roof resembled polished marble.

"Your uncle will be meeting us," said his father.

As the bus pulled into the station, Moon Feather realized that the roof was made of tin, not marble. Perhaps he would not tell his grandfather the whole truth about the capital city.

Grandfather's Tenochtitlán, the Navel of the Moon that he held in his dreams, was so much more beautiful.

CHAPTER TEN

FLOWER WARRIORS

The bus parked in a numbered slot, and the Huicholes entered the terminal.

"There is your uncle Big Tree," Moon Feather's father said stiffly. He indicated the area where friends and family waited to meet arriving passengers.

A Huichol man dressed in city clothes waved to the pilgrims. The man was very similar to Moon Feather's father in appearance, but had graying hair and a puffiness to his face.

Moon Feather guessed that the pudgy boy in the red sweat suit who stood at his uncle's elbow must be his cousin. He looked to be about ten years old.

The boy, Moon Feather noticed, had the bone structure of a Huichol, but without the sharp edges and fine angles. He was shaped of soft edges, as if his flesh was made from the damp clay of the river bottom.

Father and his brother embraced, greeting each other in Huichol.

"This is your uncle, Moon Feather."

Uncle patted Moon Feather's arm and introduced his son. "And this," he said in Spanish, "is your cousin—"

"Jesus," interrupted the boy. "My name is Jesus, but they call me Chuy, that's 'Chooeee.'" His lips formed an exaggerated pucker around his nickname.

Moon Feather shook hands with his cousin, even though it was not a Huichol custom. Chuy eyed him curiously.

"We will take collective taxis to our house," explained Uncle. "It will be faster than the subway. We live on the outskirts of the city."

He herded the pilgrims toward the front of the terminal. The Huicholes—with their embroidered ceremonial clothes, mahogany skin, black braids, beaded wrist bracelets, turkey feathers, and deer tails—and Uzra, still wearing his five hats—trooped through the bus station. People stared and pointed their fingers. Even the Guardian of the Fire felt it prudent to cover the stuffed deer head he carried with a large red bandanna.

"Why do you wear the tails of dead animals on your hats?" asked the boy cousin, poking his face into Moon Feather's. "You look strange. Do you always dress like that?"

He rattled off one question after another. Moon Feather gave no reply.

The Huicholes waited while Uncle bought taxi vouchers; then they followed him outside to a line of waiting cabs.

As the taxi snaked its way through the labyrinth of narrow streets, Moon Feather felt overwhelmed. The sidewalks were jammed with vendors selling fresh vegetables and fruit, cooked foods, clothing, automobile parts, toys, soap, even radios. People shoved and crowded every inch of space. They thronged about taco stands on the corners. It seemed as though everything one needed in life could be obtained within a few square feet of space in the city. How different from the Sierra, where one had to walk great distances to obtain the simplest things.

"Over a thousand people a day move to Mexico City from the interior of the country," said Uncle. "It is now the largest city in the world. In ten years it may be thirty-five million people."

"Why do they come?" asked Moon Feather in disbelief. His eyes were watering from the cars' fumes. Traffic hummed in his ears like a giant bumblebee.

"They hope to build a better life, just as I did when I came here twenty years ago." Uncle looked out the taxi window at the sea of slowly moving vehicles. "But I have learned that, while with one hand the city can offer wonderful opportunities, with the other, it can beat you to the ground."

"Where is the Aztec ceremonial center, Uncle? Is it near where Great-Grandfather-Deer-Tail lives? Will we pass it?"

"Tomorrow, Moon Feather," his uncle replied. "Tomorrow we will see everything."

Moon Feather tried to catch a glimpse inside the store windows as they flashed by, but his stomach was getting queasy from the cab's dodging and braking, the heat, and the suffocating fumes of the traffic.

After what seemed like hours, they entered Uncle's neighborhood. The taxi turned onto a poorly paved street lined with more of the cinder block houses Moon Feather had seen from the bus. The driver pulled the taxi to a stop in front of a gray-white one with a turquoise door.

"We are here," Uncle announced proudly.

It had never occurred to Moon Feather that his uncle might not be rich. The Aztec lords had been rich; the Spanish conquistadores had amassed fortunes. Uncle had lived in the city for over twenty years, yet his house was not much larger than Moon Feather's own *kí* house in the Sierra.

But it was well built. It would be warm shelter in the winter, and Uncle had many close neighbors.

The Huicholes followed Uncle through the gate in the rusted wrought-iron fence. Gasoline cans filled with pink and red geraniums lined the walk. The plants held their ragged heads high, warriors determined to bring a blossom of color to the gray city.

The Huicholes entered the turquoise door to find Moon Feather's aunt Naurra waiting for them.

"Welcome, welcome, you are in your house," she said to the pilgrims. She threw her plump arms around each new arrival and greeted him with a beaming smile.

"We have prepared a hot meal for you. You must all be exhausted." She tugged Moon Feather's ear with an immediate fondness that made him blush.

"Your mother must be worried about you," she said. "Such a long way from home. Now come, eat."

She led them into the small, sunny kitchen that was tacked onto the back of the house. It was jammed to its pressed asbestos roof with women who had come to cook. Savory aromas filled the air, and suddenly Moon Feather realized that he was starving.

The women quickly served their guests big plates of beans and rice, steaming bowls of rich chicken soup, and piles of hot tortillas. For the moment, the Deer-God and the mission were forgotten.

"We can eat in my room," Chuy told Moon Feather. "You are going to sleep in there with me."

Moon Feather followed him through the tiny living room, past the family altar—a table covered with a white embroidered cloth. It held four pictures of the Virgin of Guadalupe, candles, flowers, a crucifix—and four beaded prayer bowls filled with tamales.

The boys squeezed into Chuy's small bedroom and sat down on the bed among piles of comic books and posters of rock musicians whose faces were all unfamiliar to Moon Feather.

"I've never been to the mountains," Chuy said between slurps and gulps of food. "I don't want to go there either. There's nothing there I want to see."

Moon Feather did not answer.

"The city has everything," his cousin continued. "After lunch we will go for a walk and I'll show you."

The boys finished their meal in silence, then took their plates to the kitchen. Some of the adults were chatting, while the pilgrims, comfortably full of hot food, had stretched out on the floor to nap.

The boys left by the rear door, where they encountered an elderly Huichol man sitting near the woodpile in the backyard. On his lap was a plank of wood thinly coated with beeswax. The Huichol elder was making a yarn painting. His callused hands guided tiny cords of brightly colored yarns, pressing them into the beeswax to form eagles, ears of corn, flowers, deer.

"That's my mother's uncle," explained Chuy. "He makes yarn paintings to sell at the tourist market. In a good week, he can make ten or twelve."

Chuy and Moon Feather walked out the back gate and onto the street.

"I didn't know if you would speak Spanish," said Chuy to Moon Feather as they started down the block. "I thought you would only speak Huichol. I don't speak Huichol. It's a dumb language. My name in Huichol is 'Aguayuabi.' I mean, what kind of a name is that? I can't even pronounce it."

"It means 'Blue Horn,'" explained Moon Feather. He smiled. "It could be worse. Your name could be 'Aguatzaure.'"

"What is that?"

"Perfumed Horn."

"Ugh!"

They walked to the corner and turned the block.

"Do you go to school?" Chuy asked.

"Sometimes I go to a school run by the nuns," replied Moon Feather. "That is where I learned Spanish and about their church's religion. But I do not use either one when I go home. We do not attend classes in the planting season, or during fiestas. Or when we have to harvest the crops."

"I go to school practically every day of the year," bragged Chuy. "Except for today and tomorrow. I get to stay home because you came. We get summer vacation, too, and Christmas vacation, but I don't suppose you celebrate Christmas."

Moon Feather did not feel like explaining.

"I have to work, besides going to school," the boy cousin prattled on. "With the economic crisis in Mexico, we all work. My father works in a factory across the city. He leaves every morning at five-thirty because it takes him two hours to get to his job on buses and the subway. He's been working double shifts so he could have time off while you're here.

"My sister cleans houses in downtown, and my mother makes tamales and sells them at the bus stop. I work, too. I sell newspapers after school." He looked sideways at Moon Feather. "Do you work?"

"Yes," replied Moon Feather. "I work."

"Good. You would have trouble finding work here in the city—being an Indian, I mean. They won't give you certain jobs if you look too Indian. You can be one, that's okay," Chuy said, looking at the ground. "But it's bad to look too much like one." Then he perked up.

"That's why I want to go to school and get an education. I think I'll be a lawyer, or a dentist. I haven't decided. What are you going to be?"

"I haven't decided either," replied Moon Feather.

CHAPTER ELEVEN

FIREFLY LANTERNS

As the boys walked on, the houses changed. They became two stories high, not one, and the cinder block walls were painted colorful pinks, blues, and turquoises. Flowerpots bloomed behind neat stone walls, and television antennae sprouted from the rooftops. The freshly asphalted streets were lined with green trees.

Moon Feather watched a mother and two children enter their home carrying a shopping bag of fresh fruit and vegetables. He thought of his own mother.

In a sturdy house like that, she would be warm in winter. Water would run right into her kitchen, she would not have to haul buckets from the river. Food could be bought in the nearby market, she would not have to grow a garden plot.

Tutú would have a school; grandfather, a doctor. And he . . .

"This neighborhood looked like ours once," said Chuy. "But these people have been here a long time. They got better jobs and then they could build onto their houses. We'll do that one day. Our house will look like these and then, I think, we'll paint it bright purple.

"You want something to eat?" asked Chuy.

"Yes, thank you."

Chuy popped into a shop and bought a little packaged cake. He tore open the cellophane and he broke off a small piece for Moon Feather, then stuffed the rest into his mouth. Chocolate icing stuck to his hands and face.

"Let's go," he said, licking his fingers.

The boys headed back toward Chuy's house. On the way, they passed a group of teenage boys playing basketball on an asphalt playground. It would be nice to have so many friends to play ball with, Moon Feather thought.

"That playground used to be a dump," Chuy explained. "Then the government filled it in, paved it, and now we play sports there."

"What is a 'dump'?" asked Moon Feather.

"I'll show you."

As the boys walked east, the surroundings changed, but this time for the worse.

Moon Feather noticed a strange odor. The streets became dirt paths pitted by deep holes filled with stagnant water.

The houses were makeshift shacks pieced together from sheets of corrugated tin, cardboard, and scrap wood.

"Who lives there?" asked Moon Feather.

"New arrivals from the country," answered Chuy. "They come here without any money or jobs or education. That's why people call this the 'lost city.' They have to live any way they can find."

"The people's houses are only huts of cardboard," said Moon Feather. "Why don't the Aztecs see that they have proper homes?"

"The who?" asked Chuy. Not waiting for a reply, he dashed to the top of a small rise. Moon Feather joined him.

"This is a dump." The boy cousin swept his arm in a large arc.

A great sea of garbage spread before them as far as Moon Feather could see. Piles of paper, plastic, old broken furniture, rotting fruits and vegetables—some mounds of trash were taller than a man's head.

Small fires burned here and there, spewing smelly smoke into the air. The stench made Moon Feather hold his nose. The chicken soup he had had for lunch rose in his throat.

"It's pretty bad," agreed Chuy. "This used to be Lake Texcoco. Now it's just a dry lake bed where the city dumps its sewage and trash."

"Lake Texcoco?" Moon Feather stared at the ocean of garbage. This was the Lake Texcoco his grandfather had spoken of? The huge, glorious lake that once filled the Valley of Mexico? The lake where the Aztecs had raised their beautiful capital, Tenochtitlán?

"But the lagoons of Lake Texcoco were full of fish, a home for many birds and animals and plants. What happened to all the water?"

"It was drained off as the city got bigger over the years. The city grew and it filled in the lake." Chuy shrugged. He pointed to the gully of rank sewer water running at their feet. "Nothing could live in these black waters now."

Just then a little girl came by. She was not much

older than Moon Feather's sister, Tutú. She struggled along with a large orange plastic bucket of clear water. The weight of it strained her arms in their sockets, and the water splashed out, spotting her grimy bare feet.

"There's no running water nearby," explained Chuy. "The squatters have to carry drinking water from a public tap blocks away."

A pack of mangy dogs, yapping and snarling, chased a rat through the refuse. Beyond them, in the distance, Moon Feather noticed a crowd of poorly dressed men, women, and children wading through the heaps of garbage. They seemed to be looking for something.

"What are those people doing?" Moon Feather asked Chuy.

"They're garbage pickers. They go through the garbage looking for reusable things they can sell to the junk dealers for money to buy food. Things like old car parts, glass, metal, plastic, or cloth. They even sell the bones of dead animals."

How can human beings live this way, Moon Feather asked himself, shaking his head.

"These people have lost their feathers," he said aloud.

But his cousin did not understand. "Maybe they'll find some in the dump," he offered cheerily.

The way back to Uncle's house seemed a long walk. Moon Feather wished that Grandmother-Growth-Nakawé would send a cleansing rain to fall over him and wash away the smell of the decaying dump.

He longed for the clean greenness of his forests, for the high, fresh mountains and the valleys where the mangoes grew.

He slipped his hand into his shoulder bag and touched the small glass prism his grandfather had given him. He ran his fingers over its cool, polished sides as he tried to summon up images of the Sierra.

Tomorrow he would go to the Aztec ceremonial center and he would ask questions of the Indian lords there. But how, he wondered, could the Aztecs help the Huicholes save the Sierra if they had been unable to save their own beautiful Lake Texcoco? Had they lost the nature wisdom of their ancestors?

"Chuy, have you ever seen stars?"

"Stars? Sure. Lots of them—on television. Movie stars, singing stars. Why?"

"What is 'television'?"

By the time the boys arrived home, dinner was ready. An even larger crowd of friends, relatives, and neighbors had gathered in the small house to welcome the pilgrims.

Moon Feather slipped through the living room unnoticed and went straight to the bathroom. He splashed clean water from the faucet over his hands and face, trying to cleanse himself of the misery he had seen. He let the water run for a very long time.

When he returned to the living room, the house was full of guests. Aunt Naurra summoned everyone to the table.

"Come, come, the food is ready!"

Moon Feather could not resist the delicious smells of roasting chicken and pork, fresh corn tortillas toasting on the stove, and bubbling pots of beans.

Aunt Naurra had prepared his favorite dish—*cuxala*, a stew of chicken breast, corn kernels, and *chiles*.

The women placed bountiful platters of the food on the kitchen table along with fresh salsa made of chopped tomatoes, onions, and *chile* peppers. The Huichol pilgrims grabbed plates and began to fill them.

Uncle rose to his feet and called for silence.

"Would you offer a prayer for us, Brother—before we eat?" Uncle was looking directly at Plant That Grows.

The Huichol got awkwardly to his feet and cleared his throat.

"Here I am. Get me home again," he mumbled. Then he sat down.

Everyone dived into the feast. The children had glasses of sweet pomegranate punch to drink, while the men poured themselves glasses of *tejuino*, a drink made from fermented corn.

After dinner, they chatted and told stories.

"Music! Music!" someone shouted.

Uncle went into the bedroom and returned with two Huichol violins. One was painted with yellow suns, the other with two red deer.

Someone else produced a guitar, then a reed flute, and the Huicholes broke into song.

Unlike the songs of the religious rituals, this was a song of joy, a song to make the imagination flow and be one with the god-spirits. The children danced in the corner and Moon Feather clapped his hands to the music.

For a moment, for all the Huicholes, the walls of the house dropped away, and the city dwellers were once again in the high Sierra, where the wind rustled tall, scented pines and the air was like crystal.

Finally, the hour grew late.

The men gathered around the kitchen table to trade tales. Uncle lit a cigarette and poured more glasses of *tejuino* from the gourds.

"It is time for you boys to be bathed and in bed," said Aunt Naurra. She took Moon Feather and Chuy by the hands.

"Good night, boys," the men called.

Moon Feather had trouble sleeping because his head was so full of thoughts. He had seen so much in one day; he had so many questions.

Tomorrow he would ask his uncle to take him to the Heart of the One World. Perhaps the Aztec lords would have the answers he sought.

Then he had to find Great-Grandfather-Deer-Tail.

After a long time, Moon Feather sat up and looked out the window into the blackness behind his uncle's house. His cousin lay softly snoring in the bed beside him. The voices from the kitchen had quieted some time earlier.

Moon Feather leaned toward the window and looked up at the heavens. What Plant That Grows had said was true: no stars, no moon. Only inky blackness like a deep, dark hole. If the earth bucked me off, thought Moon Feather, I would go sailing right up into that black nothing, with no stars to block my flight.

He peered into the dark backyard. As his eyes became accustomed to the night, he saw—there by the woodpile—the ash of a cigarette, glowing hot. The little dot of fire moved rhythmically back and forth from unseen hand to mouth.

He watched it dreamily. It reminded him of a firefly, like those he and his father watched on mountain summer nights. The little firefly that had carried in its tail the spark that was Grandfather-Fire-Tatewarí.

Grandfather-Fire was tiny then, as tiny as the lantern in the firefly's tail. But he grew and grew to the size of a shield. Then he grew . . . and grew . . . and grew. . . .

CHAPTER TWELVE

INDIANS, BIRDS, AND DEER

"Time to get up, Moon Feather. The men are already bathed and having breakfast."

Aunt Naurra opened the bedroom door wider and entered carrying a red plaid shirt and a pair of boy's blue jeans.

"You may wear these today. The neighbors and family are lending all of you clothes to wear while I wash the ceremonial clothing you wore from the mountains. That way it will be fresh for your departure tomorrow. Was that a new shirt your mother made you?"

She smiled as Moon Feather nodded.

"Those jeans are mine," said Chuy, eyeing the clothes his mother held. "But I guess you can wear them."

Moon Feather put on the city clothes. The jeans were heavy and scratched his legs; the shirt hung loosely from his shoulders. But he was too excited to care.

Today he was going to meet Great-Grandfather-

Deer-Tail. Today he would see the Aztec ceremonial center. Uncle had promised.

"Let's go," said Chuy. "Breakfast is ready."

Moon Feather picked up his shoulder bag, making sure his grandmother's prayer bowl was inside. Then the boys joined the others in the kitchen, where Aunt Naurra was serving hot mugs of cinnamon tea and atole.

The pilgrims looked odd and very uncomfortable as they sat around the table in their borrowed city clothes.

"Chuy and I will take you to the office of the National Indigenous Institute to make final arrangements to transport the deer tomorrow," his uncle was saying.

"We know the Institute," said Moon Feather's father. "It is the government agency that has built Huichol-Spanish bilingual schools, landing strips, medical centers, and an agricultural station in the Sierra."

"And the agricultural station is full of tractors no one knows how to use," sneered Kükame.

"The Institute is helping pay the cost to transfer the deer to the Sierra," Uncle reminded them.

Breakfast finished, the men gathered their things.

"We will take the subway," Uncle said.

"What is a subway?" Moon Feather asked Chuy as they left the house.

"It's a small train that runs underneath the city, below the traffic. You'll see," said Chuy.

The entrance to the subway was a square hole that reminded Moon Feather of the entrance to the cave where Grandfather-Fire was born.

At the bottom of the concrete stairs, Uncle handed

out yellow subway tickets, which the Huicholes fed into the ticket-taking machine.

"Father, where is Uzra?" asked Moon Feather, noticing that his friend was not with them.

"Uzra came in late last night and left very early this morning to sell his handicrafts."

Moon Feather sighed. His companion for the day would have to be Chuy.

The Huicholes pressed past the revolving metal bars and followed Uncle down a long underground passageway.

"We have caves like this in the Sierra," Moon Feather told his cousin, "But they belong to the god-spirits."

Chuy opened his mouth to reply as they reached the waiting platform, but just then the subway train arrived.

Moon Feather watched the bright orange train emerge from the dark tunnel and swish into the station. It had one headlight in front. It reminded him of a giant orange worm with a light in its head—like Shurakame, the fish guide.

The Huicholes were swept into the car as the crowd rushed aboard. People jabbed Moon Feather with their elbows and stepped on his bare toes. They sucked up the air in the close compartment. The doors closed; the orange steel worm swallowed them.

What if it refuses to spit us out? wondered Moon Feather as the car began to move. Will we remain trapped forever in its metal insides as it slithers through the dark, damp tunnels under the city?

"Get off at the next stop!" his uncle shouted some time later.

As the subway train raced along, Moon Feather felt a pressure on his shoulder. Then he felt a hand tugging at his side. Someone had hold of his shoulder bag!

Moon Feather looked up into the scraggly-bearded face of a Mexican man about forty years old. He had shaggy black hair and wore a scuffed leather jacket, even in the hot subway car. The thief's right hand was buried inside the bag. His left hand yanked at the shoulder strap.

"Uncle!" Moon Feather called out, but his uncle was too far away in the crowd to hear.

Moon Feather wrestled the shoulder bag to his chest, but the man held on tightly. The thief's black eyes narrowed as he grinned at Moon Feather. His gold front tooth glinted in the light.

Moon Feather became aware of a rusty taste in his mouth. It was the taste of fear. He had never felt fear at the hands of another human being. He never wanted to know such feelings again.

The pickpocket withdrew his hand from the shoulder bag. As he did, Moon Feather caught a glimpse of a blue-green deer dancing in the fluorescent light. The robber had his grandmother's prayer bowl.

Moon Feather grabbed the edge of the gourd bowl and struggled with the gold-toothed man for its possession.

"Thief! Help! It is mine!" he cried out. But no one heard him above the whine of the train's rubber tires on the tracks.

The train stopped with a sudden jerk. The doors opened. The other Huicholes, not noticing the skirmish, crowded out. Moon Feather knew he must go with them, but he could not lose the prayer bowl. The warning bell sounded—the doors were about to shut.

Just then a strong arm grabbed Moon Feather around the waist and, with one giant tug, snatched him through the closing subway doors. Uncle had saved him, and he had saved his grandmother's prayer bowl from the thief's clutches. But his feelings about the city were beginning to change.

The office of the National Indigenous Institute was located on the fifth floor of a beige brick building a short walk from the subway station. The Indians stepped into a small room in the lobby. The doors closed by themselves. Uncle pushed a button on the wall and the room lurched and began to move upward. Moon Feather clutched Chuy's arm in surprise.

"Haven't you ever been in an elevator?" snickered Chuy.

The Huicholes got off on the fifth floor and entered a door that read National Indigenous Institute.

A middle-aged receptionist eyed them coldly. "What do you want? Do any of you speak Spanish?" she demanded.

Uncle started to step forward, but Kükame pushed in front of him.

"Yes?"

Kükame stood silent, his dark profile chiseled in granite, his black eyes smoldering. Moon Feather was worried. Anger was the sign of an unbalanced mind. What if Kükame offended the Institute people, causing them to refuse to send the deer. What would happen to the Huicholes then?

The receptionist batted her painted eyelids. "Yeees?" she repeated curtly.

Just at that moment another Mexican woman entered the office. She was much younger and she carried a briefcase. She smiled and greeted the Indians in Huichol.

"So you have come for Marrakuarí," she said, calling Great-Grandfather-Deer-Tail by his Huichol name. "I am María Elena Salazar, the Institute subdirector. Please come into my office."

She ushered them in and pointed to a sofa and chairs.

The subdirector took her chair at the big metal desk and opened her briefcase. She laid some papers out before them.

"We're very pleased to be part of this project," she said. "Tomorrow the Chapultepec Zoo will send twenty white-tailed deer to the airport. The deer will be crated and tranquilized so they won't injure themselves on the long trip.

"We will be sending you back to the mountains with them on a DC-3 cargo plane. Several charitable organizations have contributed to the cost of the charter flight."

Moon Feather was going to fly? He squirmed in his seat at the thought.

"A government veterinarian will accompany you and the deer in the plane," she continued. "He will stay in the Huichol settlement until your own men have been trained to care for the deer. His name is Dr. Francisco Calderón."

The young woman sat back in her chair. "The Marginal Ethnic Groups Solidarity Committee of volunteers has voted to supply money to buy food for the deer for two years." She paused.

"After that, you will have to maintain the animals. You must take proper care of the deer and help them increase in numbers great enough to repopulate the Sierra forests."

"How many deer did you say there are?" asked Plant That Grows.

"There are seven males and thirteen females. Some of the does are carrying fawns, so you will soon have baby deer to care for as well. Are there any questions?"

Baby deer? Moon Feather had never seen a baby deer. But he was sure he could care for one. They were probably just like calves.

The men shook their heads. No questions.

"Good. Then tomorrow morning early we will pick you up to take you to the airport. We will radio a message ahead to the airstrip in San Andrés so they will know when to expect your plane. Now, I do have some final details to settle."

She began shuffling through the official papers.

Uncle leaned over and whispered in Moon Feather's ear. "The men will spend the day finalizing the arrangements. We do not seem to be needed here. Would you like to go meet Great-Grandfather-Deer-Tail before you travel together tomorrow?"

"Of course," Moon Feather whispered back. "That is why I have come."

He had not forgotten his promise to leave his grandmother's prayer bowl in the house of Great-Grandfather-Deer-Tail as an offering for his grandfather's recovery.

"Then let's go," said Uncle.

Moon Feather, Uncle, and Chuy quietly slipped from the room, and, as the door closed behind them, they heard the subdirector laugh. She quoted an old Spanish proverb.

"Indians, birds, and deer—when they go, they go."

"We will take a taxi this time. I want to show you the city, Moon Feather," said Uncle when they reached the sidewalk outside. Moon Feather was grateful not to have to face the subway again. Uncle hailed a small yellow cab, and the three Huicholes got in.

"May we go to the Aztec ceremonial center also?" Moon Feather asked.

"We will go there first," replied his uncle. "It is on the way to Great-Grandfather-Deer-Tail's home in the zoological garden." He instructed the driver, "To the Zócalo, please."

Moon Feather organized the questions he needed to ask the Aztec lords. First, he wanted to know about Lake Texcoco, and the garbage pickers. Then he would ask their advice about how to save the Sierra. And, if there was time, he would request permission to climb a pyramid.

Only a small one, so he could tell Turtle Feet and Stinging Scorpion that he had done it.

The yellow taxi scampered through the heavy traffic; it dodged masses of pedestrians at the intersections. Soon the street widened into six asphalt lanes as it entered a huge public square.

A flagpole taller than a ponderosa pine stood in the middle of the square. From it waved a mammoth Mexican flag of red, green, and white. As the flag unfurled in the wind, Moon Feather spied the symbolic eagle perched upon a cactus. It held a rattlesnake in its talons.

"This is the Zócalo, the power center of Mexico City," explained his uncle, "and the ceremonial center of the Aztecs."

Moon Feather could hardly contain his excitement. At last he was here, in the Heart of the One World. As the taxi circled the great plaza, Moon Feather looked everywhere for the polished white marble pavement and the shining whitewashed pyramids. But he did not see them.

What he saw was a broad expanse of concrete bordered on three sides by red and gray stone buildings. A large Catholic cathedral stood on the north side.

"That is the Metropolitan Cathedral of Mexico City," said Uncle. "It was built on the site where Cortez's men constructed an earlier chapel. And that red sandstone building with the carved stone windows is the National Palace, the seat of the Mexican government."

"But, Uncle, where are the pyramids? Where is the Great Temple upon which the Aztecs held their ceremonies?" Moon Feather asked impatiently.

"You mean the Templo Mayor? The Aztec temple is there, to the right of the Cathedral."

His uncle told the taxi driver to let them out in front of the church. Moon Feather bounded from the cab and he, Uncle, and Chuy walked east, then turned north for half a block. But there was no temple.

Moon Feather saw only more colonial sandstone buildings. And a pile of rubble on the right.

"This is it," said Uncle.

He stopped before a large hole in the ground. It was filled with broken stone.

"This is the Great Temple of the Aztecs."

CHAPTER THIRTEEN

ANGELS WITH PAINTED FACES

Moon Feather stared dumbstruck at the gaping wound in the earth, at the ruined walls. Serpent heads, crudely carved from blocks of stone, still guarded the temple's remains, but there were no magnificent frescoes, no red and blue shrines atop a 150-foot pyramid. The Great Temple was a broken, empty shell.

"But this cannot be it," said Moon Feather.

"Cortez and the Spaniards destroyed the Aztecs' temple and used the stones to construct their colonial buildings," explained his uncle. "The rest of the ceremonial center lies buried under the Metropolitan Cathedral and the Zócalo buildings. What was the emperor Moctezuma rests beneath the National Palace."

"What happened to the hundreds of thousands of Aztecs who lived in Tenochtitlán?" asked Moon Feather. "Where are their descendants?"

"There aren't any more Aztecs." Chuy laughed. "Even I know that. The ones that the conquistadores didn't kill, died of disease and mistreatment. Or married with the Spaniards and other people who came after the Conquest.

"That's why they're called mestizos—'mixed ones,' because their blood is a mixture of Indian and European."

Uncle added gently, "There have not been any real Aztecs for hundreds of years, Moon Feather. Today maybe one-tenth of the Mexican people are Indian, and not all of them are pure-blooded. A few still speak the Aztec language, which they call 'Mexicano,' but not very many."

"But, Uncle," protested Moon Feather. "You wrote that you came to the Great Temple in the ceremonial center to watch Indian dancers perform in honor of the Aztec gods."

"The *conchero* dancers aren't Aztecs," said Chuy. "They're mestizos who belong to *conchero* dance clubs. They elect officers and hold rehearsals. Anyway, they dance mostly for tourists."

Moon Feather was devastated. There were no more Aztecs. Who would help the Huicholes now? What would he tell his grandfather?

"The conquerors tore down the Aztec buildings and destroyed the Indians' religious shrines," explained his uncle as they left the site. "They burned the great Indian library at Texcoco. Cortez set fire to Moctezuma's House of Birds, burning the rare birds and animals alive inside. Their death cries broke the Aztecs' hearts."

"My teacher says the Aztecs weren't all good either," said Chuy. "The other Indians who lived around the lake didn't like them and called them 'maguey rabbits.'"

"The Aztecs had been barbarians," Uncle agreed. "They ruthlessly conquered other Indians. And they offered prisoners of war as human sacrifices. But whatever the Aztecs were, they came to a sadder end than men deserve."

As the three Huicholes walked back to the Zócalo to hail a taxi, Moon Feather tried to understand what Uncle and Chuy had told him.

The wonderful island city the Aztecs created no longer existed. Its flower-filled gardens and wide canals, built so in harmony with nature, were gone forever.

Moon Feather looked at the noisy crowds jostling around him. Mexico City had become the capital of the mestizos—mestizos who no longer honored the nature teachings of their Indian ancestors.

The Huicholes stood alone now. Only they could stave off the destruction of the earth. They must return the god-deer to the Sierra. They must fulfill their pact with the god-spirits.

"May we go find Great-Grandfather-Deer-Tail?" Moon Feather asked.

The taxi driver turned onto a broad boulevard called the Reforma. It was lined with tall palm, eucalyptus, and poplar trees. Moon Feather observed that the trees were spindly, and their leaves were ragged. Some were only dead skeletons. He thought of the dead sky and the dreary houses, the city dump. His eyes smarted from fumes of heavy traffic.

"How did the city come to be in such a state?" he asked.

"From the time of the conquistadores, it grew,"

replied his uncle. "Without controls or planning. The Spaniards of Cortez hacked down the cedar forests that surrounded the lake. They destroyed the Aztec dike and clogged the drainage canals with rubble and sewage.

"Still, even a hundred years ago, Mexico City was surrounded by little villages and farms, and visitors spoke of the crystal air and turquoise skies."

"Turquoise skies?" Moon Feather looked at the gray muck overhead.

"There are two beautiful snowcapped volcanoes to the east of the city," said Uncle. "The Aztecs called them the Mountain That Smokes and the Sleeping Woman. We haven't been able to see them for over twenty years."

Moon Feather poked his head out the taxi window to scan the overcast sky. He did not see volcanic peaks, but he did see . . . His eyes opened in amazement.

"Young-Mother-Eagle!" he cried.

A golden woman floated high in the sky above the next traffic circle. She was gold-gilt from head to toe. She was dressed in flowing golden robes, and a pair of powerful feathered eagle wings of gold extended from her shoulders.

Her arms were outstretched toward him, and in one hand she extended a garland of golden leaves. His heart filled with joy.

But when the taxi came close, Moon Feather saw that she was only frozen metal, a statue of yellow bronze mounted on top of a tall stone column.

"She's the *Angel of Winged Victory*," said Chuy. "That is the Independence Monument built to honor the wars Mexico fought from 1810 to 1821 to gain independence from Spain. The *Angel* was thrown to the ground in the big earthquake of 1957, but she wasn't hurt. They say we might get another earthquake, but . . . "

Moon Feather was not listening. He was watching three little boys made up as clowns. They were juggling oranges in the intersection.

The traffic light had turned red and the taxi stopped at the corner. Moon Feather watched fascinated as the boys made their way down the line of waiting cars. They were begging for money. He was aghast. Huicholes never accepted charity.

"The traffic is too slow," Uncle told the taxi driver. "We'll get out here." The three Huicholes left the cab. "We can walk to Chapultepec Park, where Great-Grandfather-Deer-Tail lives. It is not far," he explained.

The traffic light turned green and the cars sped off, forcing the clown boys to leap to safety on the sidewalk. The tallest boy knocked right into Moon Feather. He grinned.

"Money?" he demanded, shoving his grimy palm into Uncle's face. Uncle shook his head.

Closer now, Moon Feather could see the boys were older than he had thought. Someone had clumsily painted big red and black circles around their eyes and outlined their mouths in white. The smallest boy, who looked about six years old, had his nose painted yellow.

Their pants and shirts were well worn and not too clean, and their hair needed a good washing, Moon Feather decided.

The tallest boy kept staring at Moon Feather's dark

skin and braids. "You're not from the city, are you?" he asked.

When the pedestrian light changed, the three clown boys tagged along with the Huicholes, their tattered sneakers making slapping sounds on the pavement.

"We make lots of money, me and my brothers," the tall boy said. He jangled the pocket of his dirty jeans, making the coins inside dance. "We live together on the streets."

"On the streets?" asked Moon Feather. "Where do you sleep?"

"In doorways, in parks, under bridges—in the subways."

"Don't you have anyone to take care of you? Where is your family?" Moon Feather could not imagine his mother or grandmother allowing him to live on the streets.

"We're all the family we've got," said the boy. "But we do good with our juggling. My friend there makes a lot more money though."

He pointed to a man dressed in black rags and covered with soot who was standing in the next intersection. The strange being could be the Vampire-God-of-Death in the flesh, thought Moon Feather. He gaped as long flames leaped from the man's mouth.

He was breathing fire!

"Uncle, even the grandest shaman cannot perform such a feat," Moon Feather whispered. "This man has swallowed Grandfather-Fire and can spit him out at will."

As Moon Feather watched, the fire-breather poured a liquid into his mouth, spat some of it onto the ground, then breathed into a flaming torch he held close to his face. A trail of fire exploded from his mouth. Then he passed among the cars asking for money.

"What he is doing is very dangerous," said Uncle. "He puts kerosene into his mouth to create the flames. He could be badly burned."

"Volcán! Volcán!" The street boy called his fire-breathing friend. "We call him Volcán, the 'Volcano,'" he told Moon Feather.

Volcán swaggered up to the group, carrying his flaming torch. Moon Feather took a step back. The fire-breather smiled and drew closer.

"Want a taste?" he cackled, shoving the fire toward Moon Feather's face. He leaned nearer, and Moon Feather could smell his kerosene breath.

"You better watch out," he hissed. "Men in this town kidnap country kids like you and put them to work on the streets selling chewing gum. Sometimes they poke the kids' eyes out, so they can't run away."

He laughed heartily at his own joke, revealing a black tongue and teeth that were brown and stained. Then he sauntered back to his street corner to begin his next performance.

"What he does is no spectacle of courage," said Uncle as the Huicholes walked on. "Men who breathe fire like that live only five or six years. The government calls them 'dragons.' It has tried to get them off the streets and find jobs for them, but the fire-breathers refuse to understand the danger they are in."

Moon Feather looked behind him to say good-bye to the clown boys. But all he saw were yellow-golden oranges zipping high into the air among the mass of waiting cars.

"We are almost to the park where the Deer-God lives," said his uncle.

Moon Feather could see the tops of tall green trees in the distance. A forest in the middle of the stone city, just as his father had described. There he would find the home of Great-Grandfather-Deer-Tail.

At last Moon Feather could begin his mission.

CHAPTER FOURTEEN

SISTER PANDA, BROTHER WOLF

It was a workday, but Chapultepec Park was packed with people.

"Chapultepec means 'Hill of the Grasshopper' in Aztec," explained Chuy. "In Aztec times, Moctezuma used to keep wild animals in these woods. We come here every Sunday."

Moon Feather recognized the name. This was the magnificent park his father had described, where the Mexican cowboys with silver buttons and gold braid had ridden their fine horses.

But this park did not look so magnificent to Moon Feather. Giant cypress trees, some dating from Aztec days, still stood, but many were termite-ridden and nearly dead. Like the trees along the boulevard, the park's maple, mulberry, and sycamore trees were withered from pollution. Tangles of weeds and wild vegetation covered the ground, but Moon Feather saw none of the beautiful flowers his father had spoken of.

Families picnicked on the few patches of grass to be found on the foot-worn, bare earth. Along the walk, trash barrels overflowed with cast-off paper goods and garbage. Plastic bags blew through the grass.

A family with small children ate their lunch while, a few feet away, rats helped themselves to someone's leftovers.

"They say there are two rats for every visitor in this park," declared Chuy.

Why would any visitor want two rats? Moon Feather wondered.

The Huicholes walked on through the park, past vendors' stands selling hot dogs, snow cones, fried pork rinds with *chile* sauce, silver balloons, and paper parasols.

"Are we almost to Great-Grandfather-Deer-Tail's home?" Moon Feather asked his uncle. His legs were getting tired, and every time he took a deep breath, his lungs prickled as if they were filled with tiny pine needles.

Up ahead, they came upon a murky pond that smelled of tadpoles and rotting water lilies. In the center of the water stood a small, overgrown island.

Could this be the lake his father had mentioned?

People rowed about the pond in colored canoes with numbers painted on the sides. Many rowed in awkward circles, splashing their oars clumsily in the pea-soup water. Flocks of tame ducks scuttled back and forth among the boats.

Like the juggling children, they were begging. It seemed as though, in the city, even the ducks were losing their feathers.

"I hope we find Great-Grandfather-Deer-Tail soon," Moon Feather said.

*   *   *

The sign above the gates read Zoological Garden.

"This is the home of Great-Grandfather-Deer-Tail," said Uncle.

The Huicholes entered a huge garden. Here at last were the beautiful trees and flowers Moon Feather's father had described. Feathery jacarandas, coral-flowered colorins, palms, frangipani, and magnolias grew among green cypresses and cedars.

Pink roses and yellow daisies bloomed behind clipped hedges, and circular beds of spiky red *guacamaya* flowers nestled on the lush green lawn. Sprays of peach, purple, magenta, and orange bougainvilleas tumbled from the treetops. Moon Feather wished that Plant That Grows had come with them.

The garden had been recently watered, and the aroma of moist earth, mingled with the heady perfume of the flowers, reminded Moon Feather of the jungle.

But this was not the jungle. And it was not an ordinary garden.

Immense metal cages lined both sides of the walk for as far as Moon Feather could see. Some were so high, adult trees grew inside them. The trees' leafy tops brushed against the barred roofs.

Other cages were rounded, like half a ball laid cut side down on the grass. Some pens were not made of metal bars, but of tree trunks stuck upright into the earth.

From within the cages, the voices of captive animals cried out to Moon Feather.

"Come on. Wait till you see." Chuy grabbed him by the arm and dragged him down the center walkway.

The boys came first to a pond filled with water birds.

Pale pink flamingos, snowy white egrets, black-necked swans, blue herons, and wild mallard ducks waded in the shallow water. Someone had painted the concrete bottom of the pond sky blue.

Moon Feather watched the flamingos as they balanced precariously on long spindly pink legs, preening themselves.

"I thought flamingos were bright red," he said. "My father spoke of seeing them rise in crimson waves as they flew above the Pacific Ocean."

"In the wild, they are red," explained his uncle. "That is why we call them the 'Heart of the Sun.' There they get their color from a natural diet of mollusks and shellfish, but here they are fed by man."

Such strange birds, thought Moon Feather. They seemed to belong to both Father-Sun, for their color and gift of flight, and to Grandmother-Nakawé because of their long snakelike necks and their love of water.

"Since they have never seen a red flamingo, they probably are happy with their washed-out color," he said.

"They look happy to me." Chuy shrugged.

Moon Feather saw no deer anywhere. But in the cage ahead, he did see five small, furry animals with very long tails.

"Those are African monkeys," Uncle said. "You won't find them in the Sierra. Many of the animals in this zoo were brought from places far away over the sea."

Moon Feather bent down to examine the monkeys. One little one sat all alone at the front of the cage, his small black humanlike hands and toes laced through the bars. His sensitive, gold-brown eyes looked about him forlornly, as if searching for another place, another time.

"Over here!" shouted Chuy, running ahead down the path.

Moon Feather stopped in his tracks. The creature in the next cage was not some exotic animal brought from across the sea. The giant bird was one that he knew well from the Sierra.

Why would anyone imprison Vulture-Man?

Moon Feather ran to the cage. The great gray-brown vulture, Komatemai, sat lunched upon a fallen log. The bird's huge mud-colored wings were folded about his body; the tips of their feathers dragged on the ground.

"Why would anyone imprison Vulture-Man?" Moon Feather repeated aloud.

"Who?"

"Komatemai," said Moon Feather. "He is kind and friendly. From his high mountain perch, he sees everything that happens in the Sierra. He uses that knowledge to help Huicholes less favored by luck, or those in difficulty. He never refuses a request for help."

Vulture-Man cocked his head to the side and studied Moon Feather with one big black eye.

The boy had never seen a vulture so close. Usually they were high in the sky, coasting in lazy circles on warm air currents, or roosting in a tall tree.

The bird was ash brown from the top of his head to his feet, except for a triangle of soft tan feathers at his throat. The talons on his powerful, rough-skinned toes dug into the log. His head was covered with leathery, bald skin that sagged like an old grandfather's around his massive curved beak.

"See the two slashes in his bill, like nostrils?" asked Moon Feather.

"Yes," said Chuy.

"Once, Grandmother-Nakawé sent her men on a ceremonial deer hunt. On the fifth day, one of them wounded a deer with an arrow. The vulture who lived in the mountains helped the wounded deer escape. For this, the vulture was captured, tied, and punished. The rain men pulled the feathers from his head and neck, then pierced his nose with an arrow. But the vulture got loose from his bonds and revived the dying deer. His good deed made him a hero to the Huichol people.

"How can the city people be so cruel as to lock him up in a cage?" asked Moon Feather. "How can Vulture-Man see who needs help if his perch is enclosed by iron bars?

"No wonder there are so many poor people, like the clown boys and the garbage pickers, in Mexico City. There is no one to see and answer their needs."

Moon Feather turned to speak to his cousin, but Chuy had returned to the monkey cage and was making faces at the wild-eyed little animals.

Uncle joined the boys at the next pen. They almost did not see the inhabitant, who lay sleeping in the tall grass. His furry salt-and-pepper sides rose and fell in an even rhythm, while flies danced on his pelt.

At the sound of the Huicholes' voices, the animal stirred and got to its feet.

It was another animal from the Sierra—Older-Brother-Wolf—Kaiumalli. Moon Feather had heard his cries in the mountains at night.

Older-Brother-Wolf, like Vulture-Man, was a friend to the Huicholes. In the beginning of time, he had taught the ancestors everything they knew—how to plant corn, hunt deer with the bow and arrow, cure illness, make sandals and art offerings to the god-spirits.

The Huicholes loved him because he was funny and as mischievous as a small child, half good and half bad, like the Indians themselves.

Tears welled in Moon Feather's eyes. "Why have they caged Older-Brother-Wolf?"

"For people to see him," said Chuy. "Most people here in the city have never seen a wild wolf."

But this wolf's wild soul was not behind his eyes. His bushy brown tail hung limply between his legs. This wolf looked more like the dog that guarded the sheep than the fearless predator who stalked them.

"Come on, let's go," called Chuy. "There're a lot more animals to see."

"I would like to see Great-Grandfather-Deer-Tail," said Moon Feather, but Chuy was already too far away to hear.

A large golden-brown puma paced inside the next enclosure. Larger than a cage, this pen was planted with high grasses and full-grown trees.

"The mountain lion's name is Mayé in Huichol," said Moon Feather. "My uncles fought them in the mountains for the few remaining white-tailed deer."

"What do pumas eat if there aren't any deer?" asked Chuy.

"If they are hungry enough, they come down to the settlements in the night and raid the livestock. Pumas can jump twenty-five feet in a single leap, and run fifty miles an hour. We call the puma 'Heart of the Mountain' because he is such a good fighter."

"He doesn't look so mean to me," answered Chuy. "I am not afraid of him." And he stuck a stick into the mountain lion's pen.

Moon Feather turned to his uncle. "All these animals are from the Sierra. I do not understand. Why are they caged here?" Uncle gave no reply.

The sign on the next pen said Jaguar. Two fat black cats, smaller than the puma, lolled in the shade. The bigger male cat flicked his black tail and stared at Moon Feather through narrow green slits of eyes.

The cats panted in the heat; unclean cat odors reeked from the pen. Moon Feather suddenly became aware of how hot the day had become. The blue jeans stuck to his legs and made him long for his lightweight cotton trousers.

"Jaguars are usually yellow with black spots," said Chuy. "The solid black ones are rare."

"I know jaguars," said Moon Feather. "In the Sierra we call them Tata Tari. The jaguar is the sun of the night, as the puma is the sun of the day."

The smell of hot dogs wafted from the nearby snack stand. The fat cats wrinkled their noses and sniffed the air. The jaguar was supposed to be a symbol of valor in battle, thought Moon Feather. But these lazy cats sat like old hens waiting for someone to throw them food.

What if Great-Grandfather-Deer-Tail had also become comfortable and fat with life at the zoo? What if he refused to return to the Sierra with the Huicholes? Perhaps he would not want to hunt for his food in the wild, or defend himself from predators. What would the Huicholes do then?

The zoo was filled with imprisoned animals. Chuy showed him bizarre, deformed ones: the "giraffe," a pitiful creature with spots and a long, stretched neck; the "camel" with tall, bony legs and two humps on his back; "elephants" with long elastic noses; and the piglike "rhinoceros," covered with folds of leather skin, who had sprouted two horns on his snout.

Still, Moon Feather had not seen a single deer. Perhaps the zookeepers were playing a joke on the Huicholes and there were no deer at all. Maybe Great-Grandfather-Deer-Tail had been fed to the fat black jaguars.

Or maybe he was being held prisoner. What if the mestizos refused to release him to return to the Sierra?

At that exact moment, a scruffy little gray squirrel scurried down the path between the Huicholes. His patchy gray tail bobbed out of sight into the bushes.

Moon Feather was filled with joy. Takú was here, and he was free!

The gray squirrel always appeared when the Huicholes needed him. Just as he had brought them fire from the underworld in the ancestors' times, per-haps now he carried messages between Great-Grandfather-Deer-Tail and the other caged animals.

Uncle, Chuy, and Moon Feather were almost back to the main gate when Uncle began to smile broadly. He put his hand on Moon Feather's shoulder.

"Are you ready to meet the Deer-God?" he asked.

"Yes, Uncle," Moon Feather replied, his heart pound-ing. He reached inside his shoulder bag and felt the smooth form of the prayer bowl sent by his grandmother. "I have been ready for days."

As the three Indians turned down a path that led past the water bird pond, Moon Feather realized that he was not wearing his beautiful new embroidered shirt.

How would Great-Grandfather-Deer-Tail know he was a Huichol?

CHAPTER FIFTEEN

GREAT-GRANDFATHER-DEER-TAIL

A piece of Huichol territory had fallen from the sky. The large, dusty plateau behind the chain-link fence looked like the Sierra, before Grandmother-Nakawé sent the rains. The sight of the stubbly grass and gnarled mesquite trees caused homesickness to flood over Moon Feather.

Huichol-style feeding shelters—tree trunks supporting thatch roofs—were scattered about the enclosure. But Moon Feather could see no animals eating at the hollowed-out log troughs inside them.

"Where are the deer?" he asked.

"Right before your eyes," replied his uncle. "Look harder."

A movement in the shade inside one shelter caught Moon Feather's eye. A white-tailed deer was eating hay. The boy squinted to get a better look, but the deer was far away.

"That is only one. I thought there would be many deer."

"There are," said Uncle, gesturing toward the edge

of the plateau. Moon Feather looked in amazement. He had not noticed the deep stone gully that bordered the enclosure, just inside the fence.

The ditch was filled with deer. Deer as far as he could see in either direction.

The bucks and does lay huddled in the shaded depths to escape the midday heat. Their legs were folded under them, their bellies pressed against the cool earth and gravel. Long lines of deer sat motionless, frozen like earth-colored statues. Only their great brown eyes seemed alive. Sixty pairs of moist amber-brown eyes followed Moon Feather soundlessly, questioningly.

The silence was overpowering. The spiritual presence of Great-Grandfather-Deer-Tail hovered on the soft, caressing breeze. The sight of the deer touched something deep within Moon Feather's soul. He felt a desire to drop into the culvert beside them and bury his face in their soft, gray-brown hair.

Gradually Moon Feather became aware of movement among the deer. Some shifted their weight, and a hungry doe scrambled up the bank to the feed trough.

It was then Moon Feather saw the deer that could be Great-Grandfather-Deer-Tail himself. An enormous brown stag seemed to appear from nowhere. He was standing tall and regal in the hot sun of the plateau. His rack of antlers was the largest Moon Feather had ever seen. Even in captivity, thought Moon Feather, the great stag had the bearing of a grand shaman.

"The antlers are the feathers of the deer, their muwieri," he said to Chuy. "See how grand the old stag's are. He must be as wise as Great-Grandfather-Deer-Tail."

"Are these the kind of deer you had in the mountains?" asked Chuy.

"Yes."

"Do you hunt them? Do you eat them?"

"When the deer lived in the forests, we hunted them with bows and arrows and snares, as the gods hunted the first deer," replied Moon Feather.

"My father says the deer is a god to the Huicholes." Chuy sounded confused. "Is that true?"

"Yes, that is true. The deer is the embodiment of goodness and kindness. Deer is the most sacred animal of the earth."

"Well, if they're gods, and they're so good and so sacred, why do you kill them?"

Moon Feather thought a moment. "If we are able to see a deer, it is because the god-spirits have sent it to us. The Lord-of-the-Hunt has chosen it for sacrifice. He is the spirit that protects the deer.

"We never kill a deer unless it gives its permission, and then we only kill what we need for food or for use in the ceremonies. The deer is the food of the gods.

"My grandfather says that is the cycle of life— Mother-Earth-Urianaka gives food and takes it back in blood.

"That which eats must be eaten."

Chuy looked confused. "If that Great-Grandfather-Deer-Tail goes back to the mountains with you, will you eat him?"

"No, of course not," sighed Moon Feather. Chuy was hopeless. "There are different kinds of deer in our religion. Great-Grandfather-Deer-Tail is the Deer-God-Spirit, and we are his people.

"He is served by deer-spirit-priests like the blue deer

Kauyumari, who teaches the shamans to sing—and then there are the regular deer that are to be hunted."

"Well, it all sounds too complicated to me," said Chuy. He ran off to watch an elderly zoo attendant feed carrots to a fawn.

The deer in the gully began to stir, and Moon Feather looked to see why.

A young buck with middle-sized antlers had decided to find the most comfortable resting place for himself. He ambled along the trench, routing the females from their shady retreat and herding them in front of him.

If they moved too slowly, he gave them a sharp nudge with his black-tipped antlers. What a selfish animal, thought Moon Feather.

"You are no gentleman," he said aloud to the young stag.

At the sound of a human voice, the buck turned and stared Moon Feather straight in the eyes. Its nostrils quivered, checking the wind for the scent of danger. It decided there was no threat, and the tension drained from the deer's body. The young stag dismissed Moon Feather with a defiant glance and returned to pestering the does.

One of the females scrambled up the bank a few feet in front of Moon Feather. She paused. He gazed at her and she at him. Her warm golden brown eyes were gentle and intelligent, and filled with curiosity. She showed no fear of him.

The little female was delicate and finely formed. She was honey-colored, not gray-brown like the other deer. The insides of her ears, her chin, and her underbelly were white.

Her coat was scruffy and unruly. The hairs stood up

in little tufts, as if she had run through a bramble patch. Moon Feather wanted to reach out and smooth the fly-away hairs.

Her fat sides indicated that she was going to be a mother soon. Perhaps her fawn would be the first new deer born in the Sierra, he thought.

"Why are you staring at that ugly deer?" demanded Chuy. The boy cousin was back, holding a bag of popcorn in one hand.

"She is not ugly. She is beautiful. I wish I could pet her."

"Wild animals won't let you pet them," declared Chuy. "They're afraid of everything. Watch!" He gave a shout and the doe skittered off across the enclosure.

"See."

"Deer run because that is how they escape danger," explained Moon Feather. "You cannot expect animals to think in human terms. My grandfather says you have to understand their fears. You must work with the animals, not against them. You can touch any animal if you know how to approach it. Here, hold up your hand."

Chuy shifted his popcorn to his left hand and held up his right, with the palm open. Moon Feather placed his own hand, palm to palm, against his cousin's and gave a quick hard shove. Instinctively, Chuy pushed back.

"See, you met force with force. Nobody told you to push back. Now, put your hand up again," ordered Moon Feather.

This time Moon Feather pressed very lightly against his cousin's palm with only his forefinger. Chuy's hand gave easily under the light touch.

"Now you know all you need to know about dealing with animals," said Moon Feather.

Uncle joined the boys.

"Well, Moon Feather, did you meet Great-Grandfather-Deer-Tail?"

"Yes. He is magnificent, Uncle. But what if the mestizos change their minds and refuse to let him leave tomorrow?"

"They have given their word."

Moon Feather looked once more for the grand stag. He saw him standing on the plateau beneath the shade of a mesquite tree. One more day and they could leave for the Sierra.

"Farewell, Great-Grandfather-Deer-Tail, until tomorrow," Moon Feather whispered.

"We must go, boys." Uncle headed toward the gate and Moon Feather began to follow him. Then he remembered his grandmother's prayer bowl.

"I will be right there," he called after Uncle and Chuy.

He ran back to the deer's compound and removed the gourd bowl from his morral bag. The chain-link fence prevented him from getting closer, so he drew back and heaved the prayer bowl over the barrier with all his might.

The bowl landed on its rim, rolled across the dry grass, and came to rest against a tree trunk. Moon Feather hoped that the great stag had noticed it.

"Please accept this offering as a prayer for the return of my grandfather's health," he said.

His grandmother would be pleased. He had remembered.

CHAPTER SIXTEEN

SAVAGE WATERS

As the three Huicholes left the zoo, Moon Feather looked back. He was thinking of the captive Sierra animals—Older-Brother-Wolf, Vulture-Man, the proud puma, and the lazy jaguars.

"We have a special treat for you, Moon Feather," said his uncle, trying to liven things up.

"It's a surprise," crowed Chuy. "We're going to visit my most favorite place in the world."

"Do you think we should go home now?" asked Moon Feather. He was anxious to tell Uzra about his meeting with Great-Grandfather-Deer-Tail.

"Oh, nooo," Chuy whined. "We still have the whole afternoon."

"Chuy's right, Moon Feather. The men won't be back until this evening. We have time."

"We have to take a bus," Chuy called, running ahead of them.

Ten minutes later, the Huicholes stepped from the Route 100 bus onto the sweltering sidewalk. It was early afternoon, and the city streets baked in the trapped heat. The exhaust fumes from the cars and buses gave Moon Feather a dull pain that throbbed behind his forehead.

As the bus pulled away, it left the Indians standing in a cloud of black exhaust. Even Chuy coughed.

Uncle shook his head. "The birds fall dying from the sky because the air in the city is so poisoned."

"Is no one doing anything about it?" Moon Feather asked.

"My teacher says the government and the people depend upon the Secretary of the Wind to clean up the air," replied Chuy.

The three Huicholes stopped on the street corner in front of a large white billboard that read La Ola, "the Wave."

"We're going to see the Savage Waters," announced Chuy. He was too excited to keep the surprise any longer.

Savage Waters?

Moon Feather pictured the Chapalagana River raging in a white-foamed torrent fed by days of rain.

He had seen no river in the middle of Mexico City.

Uncle, Chuy, and Moon Feather walked across the parking lot, and Uncle went to a window to buy tickets. Among the people paying admission were men dressed in odd short pants that fit tightly and left their legs bare. They wore bright-colored shirts open down the front, or no shirts at all, leaving their arms and stomachs exposed.

The women had on colorful dresses and carried

blankets, towels, and woven plastic bags filled with bottles, radios, toys, and food. Perhaps they were bringing offerings to the Savage Waters, thought Moon Feather.

He followed his uncle and Chuy through a gate and up some stairs. There below them stretched a grassy green park.

Moon Feather froze.

In the center of the lawn was a large rectangular blue pool. In it, a huge wave thrashed, helplessly imprisoned. La Ola, the Wave. Now he saw what it meant.

Moon Feather watched as the captive wave withdrew to the end of the pool and gathered her strength. Then she rushed forward, desperately crashing against the concrete walls of her prison.

Suddenly everything became transparent as a bottle to Moon Feather. The mestizos had captured the water-goddess Grandmother-Growth-Nakawé, the great blue serpent of waters that enriches the earth—the energy of movement that drives the wind and the waves on the sea.

Nakawé, the Mother of Creation, was being held prisoner in this stone pool in the heart of Mexico City.

Now Moon Feather understood why the Sierra animals had been caged in the zoological garden. The first animals created were Grandmother-Growth's protectors: the blue wolf, vulture, puma, and jaguar. The mestizos had trapped them; then they had sprung upon Nakawé when she was left weak and defenseless.

Moon Feather watched in horror as the city people taunted the great wave. Even women and children joined in. They teased her, shouting and running bravely at her when she was weakest, and riding her back on colored plastic rafts. Then they turned to dash screaming in terror when she came chasing at their heels.

The more cowardly people sat in chairs, eating and urging their companions on.

How could Nakawé, the source of life for all things, be made so powerless? She had once saved human beings from destruction in the Great Flood by instructing their Huichol forefather to make a box from a tree trunk and hide himself in it. Nakawé herself had sat atop the wooden box and guided it safely to rest on a mountaintop near Santa Catarina. Six years later, when the waters receded, the Huichol nation was reborn.

And this was how man repaid her.

"Let's go in!" yelled the boy cousin. Chuy pulled off his shirt and jeans. Underneath he wore the same strange short pants as the men.

Before Moon Feather could protest, Chuy had joined the wave's tormentors and was screaming as loudly as any of them.

"Now I know why Mexico City is dying, why the earth is dying," Moon Feather lamented aloud. Grandmother-Nakawé had not abandoned the Huicholes. "The mestizos has seized and imprisoned her, taking away her power to regenerate the earth, to make plants grow and rains fall."

Images flashed through his mind: the withered city, the dry bed of Lake Texcoco with its garbage pickers, the outlying smokestacks belching what he had thought were rain clouds—the shrinking jungle, the disappearing animals and birds, the dying Sierra.

The Huicholes would need Great-Grandfather-Deer-

Tail more than ever. They must return the god-deer to the Sierra and rally the god-spirits. But the pilgrims were so few. They had so far to go. And there was so little time.

Sick at heart, Moon Feather sank onto the cool green grass. He buried his fingers in the fresh-scented blades and tried to force up pictures of his mountains in his mind.

But the whishing, pulsing noise behind him was the relentless sound of automobile tires on concrete streets, not the wind in the pines of his homeland.

He did not reach for his shoulder bag. Even his grandfather's prism could not dispel his despair.

Moon Feather, Uncle, and Chuy returned home late in the afternoon. They were exhausted and hungry. Moon Feather ran ahead of the others to relay his news.

"We saw so much today, Father," he said as he burst in the door. "I know why the city is dying. There are no Aztec lords.

"The city people have lost their feathers. And they are spreading their destruction of the natural world as far away as our Sierra."

Moon Feather's words tumbled out in a flood. The men gathered to hear what he was saying.

"I have been to the zoological garden to meet Great-Grandfather-Deer-Tail. A terrible thing has happened. The mestizos have seized the animal guardians of Grandmother-Growth-Nakawé and locked them in cages—Vulture-Man, Older-Brother-Wolf, the jaguar, and Mayé the puma. . . ."

"Moon Feather, your imagination has gotten out of

control," scolded his father. "There have always been zoos in the world, and zoos keep animals in cages."

"But the animals caged in this zoo are from the Sierra, Father," gasped Moon Feather. "And that is not the worst. The mestizos have captured Grandmother-Growth-Nakawé. I saw her. They keep her prisoner in a horrible cement pond, in a park where city people go to call her names and taunt her."

"We will hear what your uncle and Chuy have to say about this," said his father.

But the other Huicholes were listening intently.

"That would explain a great deal," said Plant That Grows. "Grandmother-Growth did not withdraw her blessings from us. She has been enchained."

"Of course," said another pilgrim. "First the mestizos drove the deer from our mountains, knowing that without the nourishment of the deer's blood, Nakawé would be too weak to resist capture. Now she does not have the strength to escape."

"If it were true," smirked Kükame, "what would the mestizos hope to gain?"

Plant That Grows answered. "They know that Grandmother-Nakawé punishes those who deceive her, or are disrespectful toward her. She will not tolerate thieves or those who show no social justice toward others.

"She will take revenge upon those who desecrate the earth and endanger her creatures. With Grandmother-Growth in chains, man would be free to devastate the planet without fear of her reprisals."

He rose to his feet. "The world is in great peril. If Grandmother-Growth is not freed to bring the rains, all life will be finished. We must return the god-deer to the mountains as quickly as possible. By performing the ancient ceremonies, we can make Grandmother-Nakawé strong enough to release herself from the mestizos' prison."

The men spent the rest of the evening reviewing their plans for the deer project.

Kükame continued to raise one objection after another. "You are creating false hopes. Which of you is going to care for the deer when the veterinarian leaves? Someone will have to carry water to the deer from the river, at least three or four times a day."

"These are small sacrifices, Kükame." Plant That Grows spoke for them all. "The earth purifies itself and patiently grows stronger through spiritual might. We must offer the god-spirits our love and lend them our strength.

"We will do whatever is necessary to maintain the god-deer, if it means saving the world."

After a light supper, the men went to bed early. The vans from the Institute would come for them before dawn.

CHAPTER SEVENTEEN

ON THE BREATH OF
THE SINGER

*Moon Feather fingered the stitches of the red double-*headed eagle on his cuff as he waited in the kitchen for the vans to arrive the next morning.

His embroidered shirt sparkled as beautifully clean as when his mother presented it to him.

The Huicholes had been up, bathed, and dressed in their freshly laundered ceremonial clothes for hours. Now they were eating their breakfasts in the silence of the warm kitchen, each wrapped in his own thoughts.

"I'm glad you came to visit," Chuy told his cousin as he poured honey on his atole.

"I am glad I came, too," replied Moon Feather. "Perhaps you will come to visit us in the mountains."

"Yes," said Uzra, who was just joining the group. "You should come."

"Maybe, someday," said Chuy.

Uncle entered the kitchen and stood at the stove. He poured himself a cup of thick coffee and sipped.

"Moon Feather," he said finally, turning from the

stove to face the boy. "We—your aunt Naurra, your cousins, and myself—we have a proposal for you. We would like you to stay with us here in the city."

Moon Feather's eyes opened wide.

"There are opportunities here," Uncle continued. "You can go to school with Chuy. Education is important to building the future. Perhaps you could go on to the University of Mexico. Your aunt and I do not have much, but we can spare enough for one more."

No one spoke.

"You have only begun to discover city life. There are many wonderful things you did not see. Libraries, museums, great works of art, theaters. We feel you are a very intelligent boy, and you will be wasting your life if you remain buried in those remote mountains."

"Yes, Moon Feather," taunted Kükame. "Listen to your uncle. Why waste your life in those remote mountains?"

A chorus of objections resounded from the other Huichol pilgrims. "No, Moon Feather. You are Huichol. You belong in the Sierra." "Your grandfather is waiting for you, to train you in the shaman's ways." "What about your mother? You might never see her again."

"Enough!" roared a deep voice. It was Moon Feather's father. He walked to his son's chair and drew him to his feet. "It must be Moon Feather's decision. We cannot decide for him.

"Think carefully, my son. Think of what you have to gain by remaining here with your uncle. An education, a good job, a chance to be part of the outside world and the advantages it has to offer. Weigh everything carefully. What does the Sierra hold for you?"

He put his hand on Moon Feather's shoulder.

"Do not make your decision from a sense of duty, as I did. You will question all the days of your life if the decision you made was the right one."

Matzuga's eyes met Uncle Big Tree's, and Uncle nodded with understanding.

"Remember also that what you decide will affect not only you, but the children you will have. They will pay throughout their lives as well.

"Follow the deer to your heart, Moon Feather. Your mother and I will understand if you wish to make a life in the city."

Thoughts rushed through Moon Feather's mind. Here was his opportunity to go to a real school, to build a fine home for his mother—to set his own course, not follow the dictates of a life of duty and tradition. To travel the world . . .

Then he thought of the god-deer waiting to be taken home to the Sierra, of the great wave thrashing helplessly in the park. He felt the warmth of his grandfather's hand on his shoulder, as he had that early morning in the Sierra. But the hand was his father's.

Moon Feather looked deep into his father's eyes and, for the first time he could remember, he saw tears there.

He heard the words his father had spoken so long ago: "When the time comes, my son, for better or worse, the gods will turn your sandals onto the path of your destiny."

Moon Feather drew himself tall and said solemnly:

"I choose to go back to the mountains."

His father blinked and swallowed hard. "If that is

your decision, Moon Feather." Father and son smiled at each other.

Soon after, automobile horns honked. The Institute vans had arrived.

The caravan of Huicholes reached the gleaming metal airport hangar to find that the woman subdirector of the Indigenous Institute was already there. So was the government veterinarian who was to accompany them. The crated deer sat on the tarmac. Moon Feather breathed a sigh of relief. The mestizos had kept their word.

"Good morning," called Señorita Salazar. "Everything is nearly ready. Allow me to introduce you to Dr. Francisco Calderón."

Dr. Calderón held out one hand in greeting. In the other hand he held a black medical bag. The youngish doctor was slender, with a mustache slightly redder than his sandy hair. His green eyes looked kindly at Moon Feather from behind brown-framed glasses.

"The deer have already been sedated and placed in wooden crates for the trip," he explained. "I understand your religion dictated wood, rather than steel ones. Why is that?"

"The wood of trees grows from the earth," explained Plant That Grows. "It is natural, it has a soul. Steel is made by man."

The party moved toward the deer crates.

"Why are the deer drugged?" asked Moon Feather. He remembered Uzra's warning about the dangers of the poppy narcotics.

"It's for their own good," said Dr. Calderón. "The

deer will be frightened, and they might hurt themselves if they struggled inside the small crates. I've given them a mild tranquilizer to keep them calm until we reach the Sierra."

He patted Moon Feather on the back. "Don't worry. The deer are fine. Now I have some last-minute details to take care of. With your permission . . . " He turned toward the plane.

"Where is the Great Stag?" Moon Feather called after him.

"He's there—check the crates," the veterinarian answered.

Moon Feather went from crate to crate searching anxiously for the Wise-Old-Man-Deer he had seen the day before.

"Where is the stag?" he asked a member of the ground crew.

"You mean 'the Macho'?" the man teased. "He's there, at the end of the line."

Moon Feather dashed to the end container and peered into its shadowy interior. Inside was not the old stag with the magnificent "feathers," but the arrogant young buck whom Moon Feather had seen harassing the does at the zoo. The boy recognized the deer's black-tipped antlers.

He ran to find the veterinarian, who was stooped over his medical bag checking his supplies.

"But that is not our stag," said Moon Feather. "We were promised . . . " He was bitterly disappointed.

"We're sending you the best male for the job," said Dr. Calderón patiently. "The old stag probably couldn't survive such a difficult trip. Even the tranquilizer might be dangerous for him. Besides, a deer as ancient as that grandfather might not be able to adapt to the wild. He has spent his life in the zoo. He doesn't understand the dangers of the forest, or how to survive on his own. And he's too old to learn."

"Why would it be easier for the young one?"

"Even the young stag may have difficulty. I'm not sure that he'll be able to call on his natural instincts in a struggle for survival. He's never used his antlers to attack a predator, or to protect his herd.

"That's why we are sending more male deer than are really needed for this many does—seven males to thirteen females. That way, if some of the bucks don't survive in the wilderness, you will have replacements."

Moon Feather could not bear to think that some of the deer might not live long in their new home. They were all so beautiful, and his people had waited so long to welcome them.

He turned and walked down the line of crated deer, looking for the honey-colored doe. When he found her, he pressed his face against the slats of the wooden box and watched her in her drugged sleep. Her breathing seemed steady.

He reached in and petted her velvety brown nose and the soft top of her golden head. She stirred under his touch.

"You will help us save Grandmother-Growth-Nakawé," he told her. "You will help us save the Sierra, little mother."

He would take good care of the doe and her baby fawn, of every fawn that would be born in the Huichol forests. They would be the first in a new dynasty of god-deer.

Moon Feather heard his father calling him. "Son, we are ready to load the deer."

Moon Feather ran to join his father, Plant That Grows, and the veterinarian, who was supervising the loading operation. Kükame came striding across the field to where they were.

"You, Moon Feather, will be responsible for feeding and watering the deer on their journey," he declared.

"That is a great responsibility for a boy alone," Plant That Grows spoke up. "He needs the help of a man. I will be—"

Kükame cut him short. "It should not be a difficult job," he said, giving Moon Feather a cold smirk. "There are only twenty deer. The Grand Shaman called this boy a man and named him to take his place on this pilgrimage. Or perhaps the Grand Shaman was wrong. Are you not able to accept the responsibility, Moon Feather? Do you need a man to carry your water buckets?"

"No," replied Moon Feather. "I can do it."

Kükame smiled. "And twenty deer had better arrive fit and well."

"I will be there if you need me, Moon Feather," Dr. Calderón said. His green eyes hardened as he appraised Kükame. "The deer will do fine."

Kükame returned the doctor's look, but said nothing.

"The crates are aboard, Dr. Calderón," one of the crew announced.

Subdirector Salazar shook hands with everyone. "Best of luck," she said. "Let me know how you are doing."

Moon Feather stood on the tarmac looking at the open doors in the plane's belly.

"Have you flown before?" asked the veterinarian.

Moon Feather did not reply.

"Let me give you a hand." The doctor chuckled as he gave Moon Feather a lift up. The other Huicholes scrambled aboard.

The deer crates nearly filled the interior, but the Indians found space among them. Everyone was nervous. None of the Huicholes had flown before, not even Plant That Grows, although they had seen small airplanes land on the dirt tracks in the Sierra when they delivered supplies or passengers.

The pilgrims sat Indian style on the floor of the plane, precariously squatting with their legs apart and their weight resting on their heels.

Even Uzra seemed uneasy. He sat with his hands clenched until his knuckles turned white, and looked straight ahead as the engines roared and the DC-3 began to vibrate.

Moon Feather's heart thudded in his ears. He tried to recall one of the prayers to Father-Sun, but words failed him. All he could remember was the prayer that Plant That Grows had offered at Uncle's house.

"Here I am. Get me home."

The plane jerked as it rumbled down the runway, and Huicholes were tossed everywhere. Laughing then, Uzra picked himself up and put his feathered sombrero back on his head. It was the only item he could not bring himself to sell in the city.

The plane picked up speed as it approached take-off. Then Moon Feather felt a sensation beneath him as if a strong wind were hurtling him skyward into the heavens.

Once the plane was in the air, the Indians became

more at ease. Moon Feather moved to a window to look out. The city was falling away beneath him. The tiny gray buildings and ant swarms of cars became smaller and smaller. He thought of the shattered Aztec temple somewhere below, of the subway with its orange steel worm-train.

He remembered Uncle's house, the garbage pickers, the prison of Grandmother-Nakawé. He saw again the sad eyes of the captive animals in the zoo.

Each memory was like a bead in a prayer bowl, a stitch in an embroidery. The journey, like the prayer bowl, was an offering to the god-spirits.

The view changed and, beneath the plane's wings, the city became nearly invisible in a brownish yellow fog.

"Uzra, come look," called Moon Feather. Uzra joined him at the window. "That yellow grime is what we have been breathing for the last few days."

The plane rose higher into the clearing sky, and Moon Feather saw the scene below change again. They were flying over countryside. Scattered buildings appeared as tiny dots, and the trees were green fuzz upon the earth.

"This must be what Young-Mother-Eagle sees when she flies above the land," said Moon Feather. "The rivers look like silver threads woven through brown cloth."

Above them white clouds billowed. The plane continued to climb.

"Uzra, see. We are going right up into those antler-shaped clouds. We are kissing the face of Cloud-Goddess-Jaitsimura herself. I am sure she is surprised."

Like a great silver arrow shot from a giant's bow, the

plane pierced the white cloud bank and streaked into the brilliant azure sky above. Welcome sunshine flooded the plane.

The Huichol men gathered at the windows to stare in awed silence.

"The blue space," said one. "The shamans sing of it, the ceremonies speak of it. But we are seeing it with our own eyes. The ancestors only dreamed of it and accepted its existence on faith. But we are here."

"How does the airplane stay up?" Moon Feather said to no one in particular.

"I think it stays aloft on the breath of Wind-God-Eakatewari," said a pilgrim. "He is the Singer, the forever-singing shaman. I think he has whiffed us into the sky realm of the god-spirits."

Others nodded.

Moon Feather sat down on the floor of the cargo plane next to the crate containing the honey-colored female deer.

"Are you frightened?" he asked her.

He stroked the doe's ears and began to softly sing to her the songs he had heard his grandfather sing so often—calming, familiar, safe. He sang the songs of the shaman among the clouds of the blue space.

They were going home.

CHAPTER EIGHTEEN

CANYON OF THE MOTIONLESS FLY

Moon Feather must have dozed off, because the next thing he knew, the pilot announced, "We will be landing shortly. We are now flying over the Sierra Madre."

The Huicholes scrambled to the windows to watch the green pine and oak forests and the deep, rocky canyons of their homeland skim by beneath them.

The DC-3 crested the last tree-covered peak and before them lay the Mesa Colorado, the six-thousand-foot-high plateau on which the ceremonial center of San Andrés stood.

Despite the lack of rain, the dry mesa was ablaze in yellow flowers, as if Grandfather-Fire had laid out a welcome for them.

Desert dandelions, pale yellow daisies, orange marigolds, and amber sunflowers bloomed over the grassland. The saffron and lemon heads of thorny wild poppies danced among the cacti.

Even the scrub oak shrubs were covered with butter-colored blossoms. Fat young-boy bees buzzed among them, busy making rich-tasting honey.

At the edge of the plain looped a blue-green ribbon of oak and ocote pine trees. Beyond that, at the bottom of a thousand-foot barranca, the Chapalagana River glimmered like jade.

"It seems we have been gone for a generation," said Uzra.

Moon Feather could make out the dirt landing strip of San Andrés, and beyond it, a familiar Huichol *tuki* god-house.

Miniature people walked the settlement's tiny streets and some waved up toward the plane in welcome. As the plane descended, Moon Feather saw a cluster of people gathered near the landing strip, but just then the pilot ordered everyone to sit down.

There was the bump of wheels on the uneven ground and, to everyone's relief, the plane lumbered to a halt.

The door opened upon a marvelous spectacle. A welcoming committee of some seventy Huicholes waited at the edge of the field. The middle-aged shaman from Moon Feather's settlement stood in front. He was dressed in his most impressive embroidered clothing. The sombrero on his head was a mass of red and purple orchids, macaw feathers, and squirrel tails.

The men must have brought every religious object in the Sierra. Each Huichol, elegantly attired, held votive offerings—painted rock shields decorated with parrot plumes and gods-eyes woven of twigs and purple, pink, and orange yarn. They carried deerskin quivers of prayer arrows, large beaded prayer bowls, yarn paintings, and wooden jaguar heads covered with beaded designs.

Four men in deerskin costumes of the Dance of the Deer bore a shaman's chair filled with offerings of fruit, flowers, and deer antlers. The arms of the chair were tied with colorful ribbons.

"What an impressive pageant," said the veterinarian as they left the plane. "I've never seen anything like it."

He could barely be heard above the din of the musicians who played their guitars and violins with enthusiasm. The *tepu* player pounded on the drum.

The middle-aged shaman raised his hand for silence. He stepped forward and, with great dignity, raised the *muwieri* stick cascading with colored feathers to the north, south, east, and west in salutation to the god-spirits.

"Great-Grandfather-Deer-Tail, we welcome you in the name of your people, the Huichol nation. Now you have arrived in your homeland." His voice broke with emotion.

"Your absence has saddened our hearts for many years. But we take joy in our reunion. We pledge you our protection, loyalty, and devotion."

Uzra and Moon Feather left the group and went to watch the deer crates being unloaded.

"Uzra, look at the mules," said Moon Feather.

In homage to the Deer-God, the pack mules wore bridles adorned with feathers and bright ribbons. Under their packsaddles were finely woven saddle blankets made by the Huichol women for this occasion.

"Are the deer to be transported on the mules?"

"No," said Uzra. "The mules are to carry the food— look how heavily they are loaded. They will have to carry the water, too. See the clay jugs and plastic bottles on their saddles? We have to cross dry, barren country and there will be little water. What we carry with us is the deer's only water supply for the next two and a half days.

"The men will carry the deer crates on their shoulders. See, they are preparing the litters. It is going to be a very difficult three-day journey."

The middle-aged shaman appeared to supervise the preparation of the deer for the trek. The crates were lashed to the litters, each of which would be borne by four men, for a deer could weigh two hundred pounds or more.

Once all was readied, the shaman asked for his bow and a quiver of prayer arrows. He chose one and shot it high into the sky in a great arc as he offered a prayer for a safe trip:

> *"My arrow is a long-necked bird.*
> *As the sparrow hawk's heart lies between his wings,*
> *So the shaft is the bearer of my painted prayers.*
> *Feathers, guide the flight of the arrow through the blue space,*
> *Feathers, guide my prayer to the ears of the gods.*
> *May we reach our homeland, the place of flowers,*
> *The place of the rosy clouds."*

The musicians struck up a marching rhythm and the procession moved out. The veterinarian stood by, taking photographs. Through the camera lens, he surveyed the Huichol splendor unfolding before him.

"It's as if we've stepped back in time five hundred years," he marveled.

*　*　*

The orange sun throbbed down mercilessly on the Huicholes. Hour upon hour they bore the heavy deer crates, up and down steep canyons and across dry, sweltering plateaus in an almost straight line north.

"Uzra, the rains seem no closer in coming," said Moon Feather. "Look how dry and lifeless the landscape is. Do you think we should tell the shaman about Grandmother-Nakawé's imprisonment in Mexico City?"

"Why worry him more," replied Uzra. "We will explain everything when we reach home. For now, we must get the god-deer safely to the Sierra forests."

As the day wore on, the deer began to stir under the sedation, and their movements made carrying the crates more difficult. Sometimes the deer crates had to be lowered over steep cliffs, one at a time, using long ropes. The going was slow and tedious.

In the early afternoon the procession paused to rest in the shade of a mesquite grove. Some of the new arrivals passed among the pilgrims, offering everyone food sent by their village women. Moon Feather and Uzra quickly devoured the corn cakes, oranges, and dried beef.

"Dried beef isn't such a good idea," said Uzra, uncorking his water gourd. "It makes you thirstier."

"I am glad the men brought plenty of water packed on the mules," said Moon Feather.

"Still, we had better make the water in our water gourds last," replied Uzra. He took a short swig.

"I should check the deer now," Moon Feather said, getting to his feet. "They are probably thirsty, too."

He went to one of the pack mules and untied the

ropes to remove a large plastic container of water. The deer were still tranquilized, but he made an effort to dribble liquid into their half-closed mouths. He pulled some fresh green moss from under a rock and offered it to them, but the deer made no move to eat.

The drugged animals looked unnatural as they lay in the crates. Their breathing was labored and they panted in the heat.

The veterinarian walked up and down the line carrying a small bucket of water. He was examining the bucks and does.

"Are the deer all right?" asked Moon Feather. "They do not seem to be breathing very well."

"They're doing fine," the veterinarian reported. "Two or three seem to be coming out from under the sedation. If they start thrashing around in their crates, the men carrying the litters could be injured."

He took a small bottle from his pocket and poured some of the contents into the bucket of water.

"We'll give them just a little extra dose of tranquilizer. Too much could be dangerous for them. Do you want to help me?"

Just as Moon Feather and the veterinarian finished with the deer, Kükame called. The men were ready to leave.

Moon Feather realized that he had forgotten to replace the plastic water container on the mule. He ran back to where it was sitting, grabbed it, and hurriedly tied it onto the packsaddle.

"Hurry! Hurry!" Kükame shouted. "We have a long journey still ahead." He came walking toward the mule. "Moon Feather, go help the men with that litter."

The boy ran to assist the men in reloading one of the deer crates. Then they were on their way.

"I will walk with you," said Uzra as he fell into step behind Moon Feather.

As the procession reached the mountains on the border of Huichol territory, the landscape became stony and steeper. The column carefully inched their way around a bend in the path. Suddenly the mountain dropped off into nothingness below them. An abyss over five thousand feet deep lay at their feet. Moon Feather drew back from the edge.

"This is the Canyon of the Motionless Fly," said Uzra. "I think it got that name because it is so quiet, not even the buzzing of a fly can be heard."

Moon Feather listened. It was true. The Huicholes hung suspended in a vast silence.

The path snaked along the rim of the canyon and even the most experienced men walked with caution.

"Be careful, Moon Feather," warned Uzra. "One missed step and . . ." He whistled.

The Huicholes struggled along under the weight of the deer. The heaviest burden fell upon those holding the rear of the litters as they strained up the incline.

"Ayeee, look out!" Two of the men lost their balance and stumbled. They tried to regain their footing, sending a shower of loose stones that frightened the mules behind them. A mule loaded with water containers bolted in panic.

The rope lashing the water vessels to its packsaddle came loose, unwinding like a frightened snake. It was the mule that Moon Feather had just reloaded—the rope that he had just tied.

The clay water jugs and plastic bottles tumbled from the saddle and went crashing down the mountainside into the Canyon of the Motionless Fly.

Moon Feather could only watch in shock as the clay jars shattered on the sharp, jutting rocks—their precious contents exploding in crystal showers. The plastic bottles bounced from rock to rock until they hit bottom, where they split open at the base of the ravine.

Over a third of their water supply was gone in seconds. Everyone was aware of the severity of what had happened.

Moon Feather's father looked at him but said nothing. The boy's failure lay on the breeze like the odor of something rotting. And Kükame was not one to let anything rot in peace.

He stormed up the path, his black eyes flashing.

"What happened here?"

One of the Huicholes had grabbed the frightened mule and was tying the dangling ropes that had held the water containers.

"Never mind. I can see. Moon Feather!"

The boy's name thundered down the canyon, echoing and reechoing. Moon Feather felt as if he were being summoned by the god-spirits themselves. He stepped forward, ready to take his punishment.

"This is your fault. Were you not the last one to tie the ropes?"

"Yes," confessed Moon Feather.

Kükame turned to face the crowd. "I told you a child had no place on this pilgrimage. I told you the responsibility was more than this boy could manage. None of you would listen.

"Now his negligence, his foolishness, have cost us dearly. Perhaps each of you will not mind sharing the water in his own water gourd with a deer. If there is not enough water for both, whom, do you suppose, would the gods prefer drink—you or the deer?"

Blistering Moon Feather with a look, the young shaman wheeled and stalked off down the trail.

Moon Feather's face burned with humiliation. His mind scrambled to find a solution. There were still two mules loaded with water, even if their loads were smaller. If he was careful, he could stretch the deer's rations until the next night, when they would reach the river.

But the Huichol men, with their own half-empty water gourds, knew that they would all pay a price for Moon Feather's carelessness.

The procession continued to climb upward to more level terrain. The sun was its hottest when they reached the ancestor rocks. The gigantic, odd-shaped boulders sat like severed heads atop the hill.

"Those rocks were once human beings," said Uzra, trying to break Moon Feather's brooding silence. "The ancestor rocks are alive, and need food and drink. See the offerings and food left at the bases by passing Huicholes?"

"They have faces," observed Moon Feather.

"The ancestor rocks guard the entrance to the holiest part of Huichol territory," explained Uzra.

The middle-aged shaman ordered the procession to halt.

"We are entering sacred land," he said. "Bring me

your right sandals. Grandfather-Fire wishes it. I shall cleanse them, for the sandals that beat upon the earth collect the sinful thoughts and treacheries of the world."

The Huicholes removed their right sandals and took them to the shaman. He brushed each one with the *muwieri* of eagle feathers. Then he returned it to its owner.

"Now your sandals are clean. They will carry you into our holy land and return you quickly and safely to your homes. The snakes, the scorpions, and the devils of the road will be cleared from your path."

Before the march resumed, the shaman dusted each deer crate with eagle feathers, imploring the god-spirits to grant protection to the deer inside, that they might reach their destination without injury.

The procession continued in ghostlike silence across the mesa. With his feet once more on Huichol soil, Moon Feather felt better.

Two days' journey and they would be home.

CHAPTER NINETEEN

LADY OF SERPENTS

*The afternoon grew chilly. The wind picked up, whip-*ping down the canyons and across the plains as it did in the months before the rains.

"We will make camp there—at the base of that cliff, where we and the deer will be sheltered during the night," said Kükame.

The exhausted men set up a campsite just before dusk. Too tired to think of cooking, they ate a cold meal around hastily built campfires.

"The deer are beginning to awaken, Uzra," said Moon Feather as he finished the last corn cake. "The tranquilizer must be wearing off. I am going to feed and water them."

"I will help you," offered Uzra.

The two boys unloaded hay from one of the mules and gathered what fresh carrizo leaves and moss they could find. They carried some to each crate. The deer nibbled the greens, but they were more thirsty than hungry.

Moon Feather carefully measured out rations from the remaining water, giving an equal amount to each of the twenty deer.

Uzra returned to camp, but Moon Feather stayed with the deer. They were his responsibility. He felt their noses and found them to be dry and warm. Was that a bad sign? But they had had their water, and his own water gourd was nearly empty.

Then he remembered the Lake Chapala holy water in the gourd he had carried all the way to the city and back. Kükame had given part of the holy water to Uncle as a gift, but the gourd was still half full. Moon Feather ran and brought it from his belongings.

He poured some of the liquid into a clay bowl. Then he took off his blue neck-scarf and dipped it into the water. He dabbed the deer's noses with the cool, wet cloth.

"There," he said softly, "that should feel better."

The veterinarian had been watching from the shadows. "I'll be glad when we reach your settlement, Moon Feather," he said, stepping forward. "This trip has been hard on the deer. I'm afraid they aren't used to such discomfort. They've led very easy lives in the zoo."

He kneeled and patted one of the stags through the slats of the wooden crate. When he arose, he said, "When we arrive at your settlement, I'll teach you what you need to know to care for the deer on a daily basis.

"I'll leave you a supply of medicine and, if you have any trouble, you can always reach the Institute center in Tepic. They'll fly someone out to help you."

The veterinarian and Moon Feather bedded the deer down for the night, and the boy returned to camp.

"Uzra?" Moon Feather called. His friend lay stretched in front of the fire.

"Uzra?" The young man did not respond. Moon Feather shook his shoulder. "Uzra?"

Uzra removed the headphones from his ears.

"Sorry, Moon Feather, I did not hear you. These earphones are wonderful. I can listen to the radio all the way home and the elders will never know."

"Did you make much money selling your handicrafts?"

"Enough to buy the radio, gifts for my family—with some left over to buy seed corn for the next planting season. Money goes quickly in the city. Money is difficult to come by."

Moon Feather took a seat on a log before the fire. Uzra propped himself up on one elbow and looked pensively into the flames.

"I think I will go north," he said at last. "To the United States." He waited for a response from Moon Feather, but getting none, he continued.

"Many of the men I met in Mexico City go there to work illegally. They swim the Rio Grande, the Río Bravo—the river that separates the two countries.

"Once they reach a city, they find work and they make more money in a month than a Huichol can earn in a year. Two years!"

"Oh, Uzra," said Moon Feather, shaking his head.

"I could earn the money to return to the Sierra and buy myself a fine horse, and a rifle, maybe a gold watch. I could send money to my mother and sisters. And if I made enough, I might buy myself a fine house in the city."

The boys settled down for the night beneath the twinkling stars. Uzra put the headphones back over his ears and lay watching the distant flashes of dry lightning, the venom of the banded Serpent-Goddess-Ipau, crisscrossing the jet black desert sky.

The sun was only glimmering over the horizon when the shaman roused the Huicholes the next morning. They ate a hurried breakfast of cold tamales and hard tortillas.

Dr. Calderón had already sedated the deer. He was anxious to travel before the main heat of the day set in.

Throughout the morning the Indians traversed the monotonous labyrinths of ocher, green, and earth-pink stone. They crossed endless mesas covered with parched grass, barren earth, and cacti.

"Uzra, look at the clouds," said Moon Feather in the late morning.

Dark gray cloud banks rolled in the western sky.

"Yes," replied Uzra. "Clouds, but still no hint of moisture in the air. Grandmother-Nakawé is too feeble to produce the rain."

Moon Feather pictured the great wave flailing in the concrete pond in the Mexico City park. "We must hurry," he said.

The afternoon was stifling. Ahead the trail passed through a rocky barranca so narrow the mules had to be led single file. Moon Feather could see that flash floods had swept through this gorge, for large boulders of pink volcanic rock were strewn about haphazardly. Jumbles of broken twigs were jammed into crevices high above the canyon floor.

A good-sized mesquite tree had been jerked out by its roots and deposited on a ledge twenty feet above them.

"Oh, no," moaned Uzra. "Look at that."

A large mesquite tree lay fallen across their path. The Huicholes set the deer litters down on the ground to rest.

"You three, go clear the way," directed Kükame. He was looking in Moon Feather's direction, but Plant That Grows stepped forward and, with two volunteers, proceeded up the arroyo.

"Take the trunk of the tree and lift it when I say," Plant That Grows shouted to the others. "But first, let me clear away these branches."

Plant That Grows grabbed a broken limb and tossed it aside. A dust-colored rattlesnake with black diamonds on its back lay curled underneath. It had been taking refuge from the hot sun.

Fast as lightning, the huge snake struck. Plant That Grows had not heard its warning rattle.

"Ohhh!" he cried as the sharp fangs sunk into the calf of his leg.

"Snake! Snake!" shouted the other two men, jumping back.

The black-tailed rattler slithered away.

"The deer!" cried Moon Feather, as he watched the diamond-back gliding toward the crate of the young stag. The men ran and fell upon the snake with their machetes.

"Quickly, Moon Feather, help me," said the middle-aged shaman as he rushed to aid the stricken Plant That Grows.

The holy man removed his *takwatsi* basket from his shoulder bag and laid his power objects out on the ground—candles, bits of mirror, rock crystals, eagle claws and feathers, a piece of deer antler, and the dried head of a sparrow hawk.

Plant That Grows tried to speak, but his lips were already swelling. His tongue was dry and stuck to the roof of his mouth.

"I have been too long out of the mountains," he whispered to Moon Feather.

"Hand me the blade." The shaman was speaking to Moon Feather. The boy found a razor blade in a pile of power objects and handed it to the shaman. He took it and, raising Plant That Grows' leg, cut an incision in the flesh between the fang marks.

"I will send the blue deer into his body to find the poison," he said. Then he placed his mouth to the cut and sucked out the venom, which he spat onto the ground.

Wheezing coughs shook the body of Plant That Grows, made worse because of his asthma.

"The *muwieri!*"

Moon Feather handed the shaman the shaft of eagle feathers, which he passed in a circular movement over the man's head, then drew it the length of the injured leg. Next the shaman applied dried herbs and powders from the contents of the basket.

When this was done, he knelt over Plant That Grows, summoning the god-spirits.

"My gods here existing, the beginning of all," he prayed. "We know that you watch over us and nothing in human life disturbs you. Rise up on the right, on the left, to hear our supplications. Let us test if life is more than a trick."

The shaman rubbed his hands together vigorously, as if washing them. The friction produced the heat of Father-Sun. Then he cracked his knuckles, imitating the sound of the flames of Grandfather-Fire.

Next, he cupped his hands and blew into them, calling the God of Wind, who was also Great-Grandfather-Deer-Tail.

Finally, he put his palms together, spat between them, and extended his hands to the four cardinal points—north, south, east, and west. His saliva, being water, was a plea to Grandmother-Growth-Nakawé.

The shaman got to his feet, declaring, "If the god-spirits will it, he shall live."

Plant That Grows had broken into a cold sweat. His lips formed the word *water*. "Give him water," the shaman ordered.

Just then the veterinarian arrived with his black bag of medical supplies. The middle-aged shaman put his power objects back into the woven palm-fiber shaman's basket and took Moon Feather aside.

"Baiye the rattlesnake, the Lady of Serpents, was sent once before," he said softly, "as a messenger from the evil supernatural ones.

"She was ordered then to kill the Deer-God, but the little gray squirrel Takú saved the deer and led him to safety. Let us hope that Takú is here to lead us now."

Moon Feather did not tell the shaman that Takú was back at the city zoo, carrying messages among the animals.

The shaman shook his head. "If only your grandfather were here. First the water, now the snake. It is as if the forces of evil are conspiring to keep the god-deer from reaching their homeland in the sacred mountains.

"If they succeed, Moon Feather, it will be the end of the Huichol people, the end of the world."

The men returned carrying the hacked remains of the rattlesnake. It was gigantic, nearly three times as long as Moon Feather's arm. It had lived many years in this stony canyon.

The shaman took his machete and chopped off the large rattle from the snake's tail. Then he sucked the blood from the severed rattle, setting the snake free.

"This Lady of Serpents," he said, "was bewitched by the serpent shaman who serves the lord of the witches, the enemy of the blue deer Kauyumari. Now the spell is broken."

The shaman dropped the rattle into his basket. Such a trophy would produce great power.

"We will have to carry the injured man," Kükame ordered. "Make a litter for him."

While the litter was being made, Moon Feather gave each deer a trickle of the last Lake Chapala holy water. The heat in the canyon was unbearable and they were still hours from the river. He would have to ration what little drinking water was left.

"Raise the litters," shouted Kükame.

Plant That Grows moaned as he was lifted. The Huicholes set off hurriedly. As they marched, Moon Feather became aware of an uneasy quiet hanging over the barranca. It was strange not to hear the cries of the birds, or normal sounds of the Sierra animals.

He had experienced this same deadly silence

before—on the hunt. It was the silence of predator stalking prey.

"Do you notice anything odd, Uzra?" he asked.

"What?"

"The quiet."

The only sound was the wind whistling down the arroyo as it blew swirls of dust-talcumed air before it.

"You just miss the racket of three million cars on the Mexico City streets," said Uzra, laughing.

CHAPTER TWENTY

HEART OF THE
MOUNTAIN

The Huicholes trekked into the late afternoon with-
out pausing to rest. Just when Moon Feather feared
he could go no further, a green line of vegetation
appeared through the golden twilight. In the distance
lay the forested valley through which the Chapalagana
River ran.

"Thank you, Grandmother-Nakawé. Thank you,
Father-Sun," he sighed. "Tonight there will be water for
everyone."

Buoyed by the sight of the foliage and knowing that
abundant water awaited them, the men pressed on.
Working like an army of ants, they lowered each deer
crate gently, from hand to hand, to the sands of the
riverbank below.

When everyone had arrived safely at the bottom, the
Huicholes washed their hands and faces in the cool,
clean river and gave thanks to Grandmother-Nakawé.

"Carry the deer crates up to higher ground for the
night. Then make camp," ordered Kükame.

Uzra helped Moon Feather feed and water the twenty deer. As night approached and the tranquilizer wore off, the animals regained their senses.

While darkness fell, bats flitted silently above the stream, hunting insects. The men gathered around blazing campfires to prepare the first hot meal they had eaten since they left Mexico City.

They caught fresh shrimp and crabs in the stream, and boiled them over the fires in clay pots filled with river water. They toasted tortillas and maize corn cakes brought from the settlements.

"Grandfather-Fire, give our food light and power," they prayed as the food cooked over the flames. "Give our bodies strength to complete this, our sacred mission."

Uzra and Moon Feather went downstream and returned with juicy ripe mangoes, plums, and wild cherries, which they ate for dessert, along with the last of the sweet biscuits.

"I think this is the finest meal I have ever eaten," said Moon Feather. Uzra nodded as he peeled the last mango with his machete. He cut it into thick yellow-orange slices and laid them out on a large philodendron leaf.

"You finish these," he said. "I am going to go visit some of the other campfires. I want to see if there is news of home."

Moon Feather stretched out on the ground before the fire with his back against a hollow log. Soon he could hear men laughing loudly, and he recognized Uzra's cry among the voices.

"Are you alone?" The boy looked up to see his father standing over him.

"Yes," said Moon Feather.

Matzuga sat down on the log. "We have not had many moments to talk together on this journey. But I am glad you decided to go back to the mountains."

"Yes, I am glad, too, Father. I have missed Mother and Tutú and the baby. And Grandmother and Grandfather." He offered his father a slice of mango.

Matzuga laughed as he took the fruit. "I am sure they are waiting anxiously for tales of your adventures. Tomorrow we will be home at last."

"And the deer will be home," said Moon Feather.

He tossed more pine branches onto the fire, sending a fragrant shower of sparks into the night sky. The flames crackled pleasantly.

"To our people it will be as when the gods saw the blue deer for the first time," said his father. "I told you the story often when you were very small."

"Would you tell it again?" asked Moon Feather.

Matzuga lowered himself onto the ground next to his son.

"Once, long ago," he began, "in the place of songs, in the place of flowers, the god-spirits heard a mysterious voice that sang with great beauty. Search as they might, they found no one.

"Then one of the gods came upon a tiny newborn deer. It was half blue and half green. But when the gods tried to capture the little deer, it disappeared. It found a new hiding place.

"After a while the little blue deer spoke to them. 'Why do you not try to understand my song?' it asked. 'Follow my footsteps and you will find that I am on the right, on the left, in the middle, and below. I am everywhere.'

"The little blue deer was born in the blue space,

where its arrow and its offering and its candle remain. They say the blue deer Kauyumari was the shaman, that it was life itself—that it was the very rain."

Sitting with his father before the fire, filled with good food and fresh water, and with the deer sleeping peacefully on the high ground beyond the camp, Moon Feather felt at last things were right in the world.

The Huicholes relaxed about the small campfires that dotted the banks of the river.

"Let us have some music!" someone shouted.

Men around the campfire brought out their guitars and violins. The *tepu* player tightened the deerskin cover of the drum with the heat of a smoldering stick from the fire.

In the soft black night, the Huicholes danced and sang. Their music rose in joyous celebration of the nearness of home and the successful completion of the pilgrimage.

Suddenly a shrill shriek, like that of a child in agony, shattered the darkness. The scream ricocheted down the canyon, bounding off the stone walls. The piercing sound made the hairs rise on the backs of the men's necks.

For every Huichol knew that the cry had not come from the throat of a child.

The men froze as they tried to determine the direction of the sound. The deer on the hill above them, sniffing the scent of danger on the moist night air, panicked and tried to scramble to their feet in the close confines of their wooden crates.

"Father! Father! The deer!" cried Moon Feather.

He and his father grabbed flaming sticks of pine

wood from the campfire and ran up the hill in the direction of the caged, defenseless animals. The other men followed behind.

As the two Huicholes came nearer, the flickering light from their torches illuminated a puma crouched on a limb overhanging the deer crates.

In the half-light, the cat's loose-hanging gray pelt took on the form of a ghost. The puma was so thin that its ribs nearly showed through the skin. But from its size in relation to the tree, Moon Feather could tell it was a very big cat.

The puma snarled and hissed.

"Shhh! Yieeee!" Moon Feather yelled, trying to frighten the animal. Other shouts came from down the hill.

Without warning, the puma sprang from the tree limb and landed atop the crate which held the honey-colored doe. There was the sound of splintering wood. The female's terrified sounds of struggle could be heard in the pitch darkness, along with the snarls of the mountain lion.

"No, leave her alone!" cried Moon Feather. "Get away!"

Frantically he dashed toward the doe. But before he could reach her, the snorting challenge of the young stag drew the puma's attention.

The mountain lion turned its head toward the crate where the male deer thrashed pathetically against the wooden bars of his prison, in a desperate effort to free himself. His instincts told him that his does were in danger.

Centuries of blood knowledge called him to the battle.

The savage cat turned and lunged toward the crate

that held the stag. It threw itself against the flimsy wooded box with a force meant to break the back of its prey.

The wood crackled but did not yield.

Again the puma slammed its muscular shoulder against the container. It tore at the wood with its front paws. And as it did, its claws raked the back of the deer, drawing blood.

The stag butted his antlers against the slats of the crate, breaking a portion of the wood away. The razor sharp tips of the deer's antlers caught the puma behind its ear and sliced through the cat's heavy fur.

The mountain lion howled in rage. It tried to push its head inside the crate to grab the deer's throat in its powerful jaws. But the crate held fast, protecting yet hindering the brave stag in its attack.

"Yayeee . . . " By now the men were nearly upon the puma. They waved their machetes and shouted. But the starving mountain cat had the smell of death in its nostrils and was reluctant to give up its prey.

The scene was an undulating mass of fur and hair. Moon Feather could not see what was happening. He could only hear spitting, hissing, and snorting.

Grasping the burning stick he carried, Moon Feather charged the big cat.

"Moon Feather!" called his father, but the boy did not hear.

He ran shouting toward the mountain lion. He jabbed the flaming torch into the cat's back, singeing the animal's fur. The mountain lion drew back from the deer. The lion's white-fanged mouth was smeared with red blood.

For a split second boy and puma faced each other.

The light of the burning torch danced in the cat's cold yellow eyes.

"Want a taste?" cried Moon Feather. He shoved the fiery stick into the cat's face. The puma pulled away. Then it slowly retreated from the deer, turned, and ran, disappearing into the darkness of the trees.

"Dr. Calderón! Please help!" shouted Moon Feather.

The veterinarian ran to his side.

"Check the doe," the doctor ordered. "I'll see to the stag."

Moon Feather ran to the doe's splintered crate. He examined her carefully. She had scratches on her shoulder, and her ear was bitten through. But she was otherwise unharmed. The stag had drawn the puma's attack in time.

Moon Feather walked back to the shattered crate of the young buck. From the silence among the Huicholes surrounding it, he knew the situation was grave.

He watched over the veterinarian's shoulder as Dr. Calderón washed away the blood that covered the stag's coat. Deep gashes showed on the deer's back and shoulders. Blood covered his throat, but it was the blood of the puma, not the deer.

The young stag's head lay at a strange angle, his neck twisted unnaturally. The veterinarian rose.

"His wounds are severe, Moon Feather. But the real damage the deer did to himself when he thrust so hard against the crate. It's very serious, I'm afraid. I'll stay with him through the night."

Moon Feather looked down at the stag's wild eyes, his heaving sides.

"I am sorry I had such bad thoughts about you when

I first saw you teasing the does in the zoo," he said. "You were arrogant then, and boastful. But tonight you proved that you have a valiant heart and the courage of Kauyumari, of Great-Grandfather-Deer-Tail himself."

Moon Feather prayed to the god-spirits that the young deer would live to run free in the Huichol forests with his offspring. If the gods could not save the stag's life, perhaps the veterinarian's Spanish medicine would.

With his eyes glued to the broken crate, Moon Feather sat in the darkness beneath the crystal tears of stars—until the Morning Star Tonoami appeared in the eastern sky to protect Father-Sun as he ascended from the underworld.

CHAPTER TWENTY-ONE

CANDLE OF LIFE

The men worked before daylight to repair the young stag's wooden crate and lash it to a litter. Uzra and Moon Feather watched the deer as he lay quietly, breathing rhythmically under the sedation the veterinarian had given him.

"He'll be all right," said Dr. Calderón. "He is young and strong."

Just at dawn, the middle-aged shaman called the men together. "Bring the stag to the edge of the river," he ordered.

As the first rays of yellow sun broke into the canyon and fell upon the crystal water of the river, the shaman lifted the *muwieri* shaft with its eagle feathers and sang a salute to the four cardinal directions.

He sang to the sky above, where Father-Sun was rising. He sang to the earth below, where Mother-Earth-Urianaka bubbled forth the sweet spring of life. Kükame stood beside him, holding a burning candle.

The shaman dipped the *muwieri* into the river, then sprinkled the injured deer with the healing water of life.

The sun moved higher, and the shaman raised the feathered shaft as if capturing the sunbeams dancing in the morning sky. He dusted the wooden slats of the deer's crate with it, imparting to the stag inside the life force of the sun.

Then the shaman took a beeswax candle and lit it from the one held by Kükame. As he did so, he prayed to the god-spirits:

"We know that everything has a beginning,
The sacred candle of life is lit one from another
As life and knowledge are passed from one generation to the next."

He touched the injured deer with his hand.

"Attend now, oh gods, the sacred candle of life. The spirit of Great-Grandfather-Deer-Tail is among us. It dwells here, in the broken form of this humble vessel.

"Today it appears that this flower is going to lose its color. My gods, do not forsake him.

"My gods who abide in the sacred mountains, do not scorn our prayers. Do not blow out the candle of life."

The shaman knelt and stuck the burning candle into the sand of the riverbank. It continued to burn, flickering in the breeze, as the Huicholes regrouped and prepared to complete the final leg of their journey.

*   *   *

The procession waded the river at its lowest point, Los Puentitos, the "Little Bridges."

"We are lucky the water is still low," said Uzra. "Once Grandmother-Growth-Nakawé is freed and brings the rains, the Chapalagana River will rampage and flood, and this canyon will be impassable."

The last hurdle was the climb from the river valley to the plateau above. Then only a few deep canyons and mountain mesas separated the Huicholes from their home.

"Gently, gently," cautioned the middle-aged shaman as the men hoisted the crate of the young stag. They handled it as if it contained one of their own children.

At the summit, they waited for the veterinarian to examine the wounded buck.

"He's holding his own," Dr. Calderón advised Moon Feather, "but we must reach the settlement as soon as possible."

The pilgrims struck out across the highland mesa. A sparrow hawk wheeled soundlessly above them in the clear blue sky. Again Moon Feather noticed the uncanny muteness of the landscape. The birds, even the raucous sparrow hawk, were strangely silent. Had he lost his hearing in the city?

Ahead of the column, the trail forked upon reaching a narrow, rocky canyon. The fork to the right skirted the edge of the canyon, then crossed an open meadow. The path to the left descended and passed directly through the canyon itself.

Kükame halted the procession, and the men took the opportunity to rest from the weight of the litters.

"We shall take the canyon route," declared Kükame. "It is faster and shorter by several miles."

The middle-aged shaman objected. "The canyon is too narrow and difficult to travel with the deer. The upper route may be longer, but the walking will be easier."

"Time is of the greatest importance," argued Kükame. "The deer and one of our men are injured. I say we go by way of the canyon."

"It is urgent that the god-deer reach the settlement," the men agreed. "Take the shorter way."

The middle-aged shaman conceded to Kükame, and they resumed the journey, taking the lower canyon trail.

The column was forced to snake into single file as the men picked their way along the rock-strewn path. The crunch of their footsteps on the gravel was the only sound. The canyon seemed endless to the men as they struggled in the dusty heat.

Some places were so narrow that there was barely room for the deer crates to pass between the boulders. They had stopped to hoist a crate over a large boulder when . . .

Crack! Whingg! Crack!

"Firecrackers!" Moon Feather cried to Uzra when he heard the noise. "A celebration. The villagers must be coming to meet us."

Pock!

A shower of small rocks exploded from a spot on the canyon wall just to the right of Moon Feather's elbow.

"Firecrackers?" shouted Uzra, ducking behind

a boulder. "Those are bullets. Someone is shooting at us!"

Rifles barked overhead. Moon Feather looked up to see puffs of white smoke along the top of the ridge above them. The Huicholes stopped, confused. Some set down the deer litters.

"Leave the deer," cried Kükame. He rushed along the line of marchers. "Leave the deer and run for your own lives."

Puffs of dust rose where bullets slammed into the earth near the deer crates. The Indians stood firm.

"Run, run," shouted Kükame. He grabbed a Huichol man by the arm. "You are not their target, the deer are. Leave the animals. They are not worth dying for!"

The Huicholes understood only that someone was threatening to kill the god-deer they had struggled to bring this far.

"Great-Grandfather-Deer-Tail is in danger," cried the middle-aged shaman, wringing his hands. "Our wives, our children, our parents wait ahead for the salvation of the Deer-God-Spirit. What will happen to the world if the god-deer do not reach the Sierra? What will happen to our people?"

"What will happen to Grandmother-Nakawé?" asked Moon Feather, remembering the thrashing wave.

The shots continued. The bullets came frighteningly close now as the shooters honed in on their targets from the distance. Something whanged past Moon Feather's ear.

A cold calm settled over the Indians. They set the remaining deer litters on the ground. In spite of the bullets raining around them, they stood rooted.

Without a word, Moon Feather's father stepped forward and placed himself before one of the crated deer. As if on an unspoken command, the other Huicholes followed—Uzra, the middle-aged shaman, the litter bearers. Armed only with the machetes they carried in their belts, they formed a human barrier to protect the god-deer.

The sense of unity was contagious. Even though Moon Feather was terrified, he went to stand beside his father. If he was going to die, he would die for the Huichol nation.

"No, no, you will be killed," Kükame yelled as he tried to push the men aside. "Leave the deer!"

"Ohhh!"

Moon Feather's father cried out in pain as a crimson stain spread on the shoulder of his embroidered shirt.

Matzuga bent and clutched his arm. He staggered, but he did not fall.

"I did not mean for this to happen," Kükame cried at the sight of the red blood.

He waved his arms and shouted toward the ridge above the canyon. "Stop, stop, you said no one would be hurt! We were only to prevent the deer from reaching the Sierra!"

A bullet zinged into the dust at his feet.

Then, as suddenly as the firing had begun, it ceased. The silence reverberated in the ears of the Huicholes as loudly as the shots.

Someone shouted above them. The Huicholes looked up to see the tenant farmers standing on the canyon's rim. They were waving rifles and motioning for the Indians to move on. The burly farmer with the big black mustache was among them.

The tenant farmers were holding three prisoners bound with ropes—three mestizo men dressed in blue jeans and straw hats. One of the mestizos wore a red shirt.

"The shooters are the mestizos who were working the poppy fields," said Uzra. "Don't you recognize the shotgun? They were trying to keep us from reaching the Sierra with the god-deer," Uzra explained to Moon Feather. "They knew if the deer failed to arrive, our people's will would be broken. Kükame could convince them to give up the rights to our land. Then the mestizos could grow all the poppies they wanted in the Sierra valleys."

"You mean Kükame was working with them? He led us into this ambush?" Moon Feather was shocked.

"Ask him."

Uzra looked coldly at the young shaman who stood with his head down, his hands at his sides. "Kükame has fallen like a moth into the flames of his own treachery."

The last miles of the journey passed without incident. The breathing of the young stag was shallow but steady. The veterinarian had insisted Matzuga ride one of the pack mules, even though his shoulder wound was not serious. Kükame trailed far behind at the end of the column, his deceit known to all, his disgrace sealed. The council of elders would decide if banishment would be his fate.

As the Huicholes climbed into the mountains, the

land became greener once more. The terrain was familiar and welcoming.

Wind rustled in the tall sunlit crowns of the ponderosa pines, carrying their fresh pine-vanilla scent to the tired pilgrims. White-throated robins and meadowlarks tweeted across the grassland mesas; sparrow hawks and red-tailed hawks lazed in the azure sky above emerald green forests.

The pilgrims saw everything with new eyes. How clean, how alive, how serene were their Sierra Madre.

"Is it possible we have only been gone one week?" Moon Feather asked Uzra.

"It seems like a hundred years have passed," agreed Uzra.

The weary procession of Indians made quite a sight as they trudged across the last dusty plateau: litter bearers carrying the twenty deer crates, Plant That Grows upon his litter, Moon Feather's father riding in his bloodstained shirt, the worn-out Huicholes burdened with religious paraphernalia, including the shaman's chair, yarn paintings, and the stuffed deer's head still faithfully carried by the Guardian of the Fire.

From the top of the final rise, they gazed down upon the small plain below, where their adobe and stone houses sat. Tendrils of pale gray cooking smoke spiraled above the thatched roofs. Black smoke rose from the bonfire blazing in the central patio. The women would no longer need to keep it fed. Their men had returned.

Children of the settlement had been keeping a lookout for them, and, when they saw the outlines of the returning pilgrims atop the hill, they waved and broke into shouts of joy.

Some of the little boys sped off in the direction of the plaza to announce the procession's arrival. Moon Feather's friends dashed across the mesa and scrambled up the stony path to meet him.

"Did you bring Great-Grandfather-Deer-Tail? Where is he?" Stinging Scorpion, Sound of Water, and Reed Grass swarmed around him. "Did you have any adventures?"

Moon Feather did not know where to begin, so he just nodded.

Turtle Feet came running up. "Where is my father?" he demanded. "I do not see him." Moon Feather did not reply.

Stinging Scorpion took the empty holy water gourd from Moon Feather's shoulder. "Let me help you."

It took some time for the Huicholes to descend the slippery zigzag path. By that time the entire settlement was aroused, and a stream of people came running to escort the pilgrims.

The women and children brought armloads of flowers and offerings to welcome Great-Grandfather-Deer-Tail. Little girls ran alongside the crates, decorating them with garlands of purple asters and yellow marigolds. They wove the stems of many-colored flowers through the crates' wooden slats.

They craned their necks to peek at the deer inside. Most of them had never seen a live deer.

Ahead, in the settlement, a welcoming delegation of elders awaited the pilgrims' arrival. Moon Feather could make out their richly embroidered ceremonial clothing, their feathered sombreros, and their red, flannel-edged capes.

Three shamans, proudly erect, stood before the bonfire of Tatewarí that remained burning in the plaza. Two were black-haired and tall.

The shaman in the center was a small, elderly man. Moon Feather recognized the mane of iron gray hair.

The Grand Shaman, Moon Feather's beloved grandfather, was waiting to welcome them. Great-Grandfather-Deer-Tail had answered his prayer.

CHAPTER TWENTY-TWO

SONG OF
THE BLUE DEER

The settlement churned with boisterous activity by the time the procession arrived. Horns blew and a chorus of hoots and whistles greeted the pilgrims as they paraded toward the central plaza. In joyous celebration, the music of guitars and violins filled the air, punctuated by the shish of gourd rattles and the beat of the *tepu* drum.

Everyone rushed to greet the returning heroes. The men were dressed in their most colorfully embroidered clothes. The women wore red petticoats and bright flowered blouses. They wore flowers woven in their hair, and on their bosoms bobbed necklaces of turquoise beads and seashells.

Men had painted red and yellow prayer signs on their faces while the women pasted white *totó* flower blossoms to their cheeks.

The air was rich with the smells of roasting beef and fresh corn dough toasting.

As the pilgrims approached the three shamans, Moon Feather's grandfather beamed at the men. He was happy to see his grandson return safely and with success.

"Welcome, pilgrims," he said. "Welcome to the spirit of Great-Grandfather-Deer-Tail. You have returned to your home. Your people wait to serve you. May you see that the greatest happiness that can throb in our hearts is to feel your presence among us, your submissive servants."

He motioned for the pilgrims to come forward.

"Are the deer well? How have they fared on their journey?" He looked at the bloody stain on Matzuga's shirt. "I want to know everything, but first, open the crates and let us greet the god-deer."

The men set the litters down and unlashed the crates. They pried open the first two, and the brown-gray deer inside tottered out into the sunlight. The groggy animals blinked their eyes.

The crowd cheered and applauded.

Moon Feather's words bubbled out excitedly as he told his grandfather of the pilgrims' adventures and the valiant battle the young stag had waged against the puma.

"Well, well, what a story!" exclaimed the Grand Shaman. "Come, we shall go meet this brave stag together. I must welcome this courageous deer."

They walked to the stag's crate, which sat decorated with yellow primroses.

"Open it and let us greet the great Deer-God-Spirit in the name of his people," said Moon Feather's grandfather.

Two Huichol men forced open the wooden slats and stood back. A cry went up from the people standing nearby.

The young stag was dead.

"What is it?" Moon Feather pushed through the crowd and reached the crate. "No," he choked.

Tears surged silently down the boy's face as he looked at the still deer. He wept, not only for the death of so magnificent an animal, but because he, Moon Feather, had failed. Failed his grandfather and the Huichol world. The welfare of the deer had been his responsibility.

He felt an arm around his shoulder and he looked up into his father's eyes. His father held him as he sobbed.

Moon Feather's grandfather said nothing. He motioned for the other crates to be opened.

Two more male deer were dead.

The Grand Shaman bent to examine the dead deer while the does and the remaining four bucks were herded into the new corral that had been built for them.

When the old shaman rose, his face was sad and his voice was gentle.

"Great-Grandfather-Deer-Tail has given us the sacrifice of three of the finest white-tailed deer as a sign that he has returned to the Sierra, and that he is pleased.

"We are to use his gifts of the deer in the ancient ceremonies. Each of the three main settlements will be given one of the deer sacrifices. Let us feast and welcome him with joy."

The people stood silently.

"Our brave men," continued the Grand Shaman, "have dared the dangers of the natural and unnatural worlds to bring the god-deer to us. Let us not feel sadness for the stags who did not survive. Their spirits are

god-spirits would renew their blessings upon the world.

Just as the great stag had died, Moon Feather knew his grandfather would one day pass away. The mantle of responsibility for the Huicholes' survival would fall upon the shoulders of another.

Perhaps one day he, Moon Feather, would become Grand Shaman, as his grandfather had been. Kauyumari would appear in a dream to him as a newborn deer to tell him he was chosen.

He would see the five deer running—blue, red, yellow, green, and white. The deer would talk to him and teach him the shaman's songs.

He knew now that was the Huichol reason to be—to serve as caretakers and guardians of their culture, the legacy left them by their ancestors, and to pass it on to their descendants.

Moon Feather watched the doe drop her head to nibble the green grass. As her fawns would grow to be strong deer and repopulate the forests, his own children would one day be born to guard and inherit the Huichol land.

Moon Feather would return to school. Perhaps he would go to study at the university in Guadalajara. He would learn all that the Mexicans and Mexican law and medicine could teach him in order to help his people.

But never would his heart yearn for the land beyond the mountains.

The cry of a golden eagle in flight drew his eyes upward. Young-Mother-Eagle soared aloft in the Sierra sun.

"Welcome home, Moye' li Metzaya," she seemed to say. "The candle burns bright."

AFTERWORD

Two months after the white-tailed deer were returned to the Sierra Madre, the Huichol Indians received word that a great earthquake had struck Mexico City.

In the letter Chuy wrote describing the event, he told how the buildings had begun to sway, slowly at first, then gaining a circular momentum.

Stronger and stronger had come the earthquake, until whole buildings collapsed. Thousands of people were killed and many more were injured.

Much of the water had been thrown from the pool at La Ola, Chuy wrote.

The Huicholes nodded solemnly as they heard the news. They grieved for those who had lost their lives. But such were the laws of the natural world, they added, shaking their heads.

"Grandmother-Growth-Nakawé punishes those who deceive her, or are disrespectful toward her creations."

Grandmother-Growth was free.

AUTHOR'S NOTE

So Sings the Blue Deer is based upon a true story. While Moon Feather and the other characters are fictional, and some incidents were created for drama, the Huichol Indians did make a journey to Mexico City to bring white-tailed deer back to the Sierra Madre. Three male deer did die on the return.

Two years after the deer project was first conceived, the Huichol Indians were awarded the National Ecology Prize of Mexico by then President Miguel de la Madrid Hurtado for their efforts to repopulate the Sierra Madre Occidental forests with white-tailed deer.

The government of the state of Nayarit, Mexico, has now signed an agreement with the Cousteau Society, headed by Captain Jacques-Yves Cousteau and his son Jean-Michel Cousteau, which is called the Master Plan for Tourism and Ecological Development of the state of Nayarit. It will assure that the environmental integrity of the coastal areas and the territory of the Huichol Indians will be safeguarded.

In the devastating aftermath of the Mexico City earthquake, a new unity was born among the city dwellers. And a new environmental awareness developed. Although much work remains to be done, environmental groups organized by the city's adults and children, are beginning to make a difference. Programs are being initiated to clean up what is now the largest and still the most polluted city in the world.